Leaving
New Orleans

BY
MARCUS OWENS

Grimes One Media
Atlanta

Leaving New Orleans   Marcus Owens

Leaving New Orleans

www.leavingneworleans.net

ISBN-13: 978-0991335121
ISBN-10: 0991335120

Published by Grimes One Media

Cover Design by Kermin Middleton

Copy Editing by Susan Shepherd, and Monica San Nicolas

The Reviews Are In

"Certainly riveting" – Monica San Nicolas

"A masterful picture with words" – Antonio Smith – 215 Entertainment

"An emotional ride that will leave you speechless"- Grimes One Media

"Five stars hands down, excellent book" – Adinerado Dec

Contents

Preface

After watching a tragic disaster occur within America, I was inspired to write a love story. The overall thought was to be a compelling movie script that involved a young lady who is displaced from home, and finds herself alone in a very unfamiliar place. As the idea brewed, the title "Leaving New Orleans" became the centerpiece for the story. While vacationing in New Orleans for several days, the story came together and was even clearer to me. After taking several notes of streets and landmarks, I wanted to convey the story in its purest form. My objective was to paint a vivid picture with words that could touch the emotions of the reader and make the story surreal. I wanted my readers to feel like they are part of Angela's experience.

As the story formed, each character started to take life of their own and different personalities took shape to make the story flow from begging to end. From Angela's ride home from work while talking to her best friend Christy, who is an Army brat, to her sharing time with her mother, Ellyn Johnson, each character has a personality of their own to make the story interesting. The plot centers around Angela, the main character, whose life experience growing up in New Orleans Lower 9th Ward is turned upside down in one day by a horrible tragedy that sends her life into complete turmoil. Angela experiences a set of emotional rollercoaster rides throughout the story, but in the end, she discovers the true meaning of life, love, and relationships.

Chapter 1 - The Way Home

*J*uly 1, 2004

*I*t's a hot summer day in the city of New Orleans, and Bourbon Street is alive and swinging. The rich smells of Cajun cooking—gumbo, steamed oysters, and red beans and rice—spill onto the sidewalk from restaurants and homes, and even though the windows in my car are rolled up, I can hear jazz music playing as I slowly pass through the everyday excitement of the city. Interrupted by hundreds of pedestrians walking across the street in front of my car, the constant stopping and going is a nightmare in this heat. It's hot as hell, and I don't have a working A/C in my car. *Beep, Beep!!* I blow my horn in rage hoping they would move, "Get the hell out the way!" I yell out the window. *Beep, Beep!!* After a long day at work, I'm not in the mood. It's too damn hot for this. "Hit me if you want to bitch, you in that much of a rush, you should've took your ass another way!" the pedestrian yells. *Beeeeeeeeeeeep!!!* "Fuck you, now get the fuck out the way before I do hit your ass!!! It's too damn hot out here to be fucking playing!" The pedestrian grabs his crotch and gives me the middle finger, "No, fuck you!!!" Disgruntled, hot, horny, hungry, and I have a headache that just want let up, now isn't the time. I'm sweating like crazy, too. What a combination. This has to be one of the worst days of my life. I can't wait to get home.

It's hot, almost vibrantly hot, and humid, with seemingly no end in sight. Last night the weatherman spoke of rain, but it won't come until Saturday or Sunday, and I'm sure before the weekend arrives the temperature will climb up into the nineties. With the humidity, New Orleans' heat will be just as dangerous as it would be anywhere else in the South. We'll get highs in the upper nineties that feel like a hundred degrees. But in spite of the weather, the city's four hundred and sixty thousand residents are going on with life at their normal pace, enjoying the incredible ambience of the city.

Despite the heat, I love the city of New Orleans. This is my hometown. I was born at Sheffield Memorial Hospital and raised on Gordon Street in the Lower 9th Ward, where I live with my momma and my younger brother Mark.

I don't see my brother much, though. He works the night shift as a forklift driver at a local furniture warehouse, and since he gets off work just as I'm leaving for my own job, I'm usually gone by the time he arrives. I only see him once or twice a week, when he comes home from shacking up with one of his many girlfriends to get some clean clothes. Mark is twenty-three now, and sometimes he acts like he's God's gift to women. Granted, he does have the family Creole genes, and some women fall head over heels for him. But he still shouldn't let his boyish looks get the better of his personality the way he does.

Growing up, Mark and I were as close as siblings could be. Like any sister and brother, we've had our good times and our bad times, but we've always been fiercely loyal. Once, two girls from my neighborhood took a dislike to me and decided to fight me just because they could, being a year older and bigger, with me still in the fifth grade. It was my first fight, and I already knew I was going to lose, but I knew that if I didn't fight it would be worse, so I held my ground as they approached.

Out of nowhere, Mark came running up with this mean look on his face and his hands curled up in fists. He was six or seven, but when he shouted, "Y'all better leave my sister alone!" I couldn't help but feel a bit more confident. He was more funny and cute than scary, but I still felt better about going into the fight knowing he had my back.

Did we win the fight? Hell, no! We got our butts kicked. But the girls didn't try to fight me again after that, and I learned that my little brother would fight for his big sister. After that fight, we were a team.

My momma, Ellyn Johnson, is tough. She's sixty-eight years old and every bit of five feet five inches tall, but she often behaves like she's forty.

When I was four years old, only three years after Momma and Daddy moved to the Lower 9th Ward from Arkansas, Daddy left. He just got up and left one day, never to return. So, Momma was left to raise us on her own. I never understood why he left her to struggle so hard to raise us, but he did. And you'd best believe Momma was mad as hell. I was mad, too, but I was hurt more than anything. To me, he was my daddy and I was his little girl. I didn't understand how he could leave his family like that.

Momma, though, wanted to kill Daddy for leaving her to take care of everything by herself. I'd never seen Momma so angry at somebody. And she was eight months pregnant with my brother Mark. When he was born, things got tough and Momma had to get a second job. She would get up to go to work at sunup every day, to bring home barely enough money to keep food on the table and a roof over our heads. How she managed, only God knows, but somehow she did it.

I can remember when Momma would send me to buy food at Green's Grocery Store on the corner of Tupelo

Street. Mr. Green, a sweet Asian man in his mid-fifties, would sometimes give Momma food on credit to take home when times were especially hard for us. He knew he could count on Momma to come to the store in a week or two to cash her paycheck and pay back the money she owed him. Sometimes, when he knew we were really struggling, he wouldn't take her money at all. Mr. Green was our lifesaver several times when we didn't have much to eat.

Not only was he our lifesaver, but over the years he became a lifesaver to a lot of people in the neighborhood who were in need of groceries but temporarily short of cash. It was heartbreaking to learn, more than a decade later, that someone had killed him during a botched robbery. When Mr. Green was murdered, it saddened the community, but it also brought us all together. We held a rally in support of a good man who had helped to build up the community he loved, and we expressed our deepest sympathies to his family by holding a candlelight vigil in his honor. Green's Grocery Store had been a cornerstone in the Lower 9th Ward for many years, and his contributions to the neighborhood, marked by countless caring deeds, had not gone unnoticed. It was only fitting for us to show our support.

After the botched robbery and murder of Mr. Green, Mr. Green's family wanted to close the store, but the community fought to keep it open. We spoke to the family about how much we needed them, and told them truthfully that the Lower 9th Ward wouldn't be the same community without them. To remind them that we were, in many ways, a happy extended family, many of our neighbors contributed pictures of their families posing with Mr. Green and his family. Many of the pictures were of happy moments taken during parties and gatherings. A few of them showed Mr. Green's children and their friends standing together outside the store.

Eventually, we were able to convince the family of how much they'd meant to the neighborhood over the years, and the show of love and support helped to change their minds about leaving the neighborhood. It was a tragic time, though, and one I'll never forget. Mr. Green died shortly before Christmas, which brought back some childhood memories of my own. Although my situation had been far less tragic, I had still felt the pain of the Green family. Never again would they be able to share Christmas together as a family. And for years, it had been painful not to have my daddy around so we could celebrate the most wonderful time of the year together as a family. The only difference was that Daddy chose to leave his family, and Mr. Green didn't make that choice. Two different situations, but they were both painful in their own way.

I'll never forget the Christmas of '85. Mark was just four years old then, and I was eight. Momma seemed to struggle particularly hard that year, and giving us some kind of Christmas was really challenging. Momma got so desperate she hunted Daddy down and tried to make him meet his financial obligations. It almost worked too, but he backed out just two days before Christmas because of other so-called "obligations."

She caught herself preparing us for heartbreak by telling us not to expect too much under the tree, and she couldn't bear our disappointment. So, she did what she thought she had to do and sacrificed some of the rent money to buy what presents she could at the local five and dime store in our neighborhood.

We had a nice Christmas that year, in spite of Dad and his "obligations." Everything Mark and I asked for, Momma made every attempt to get. I could tell that for once, she didn't care about Dad or about the rent money, just from watching her smile as Mark happily opened a present. I don't remember any of the gifts I got that year, but I do remember seeing Mark and Momma happy. The Christmas gifts weren't important; what made that Christmas special was that we were all together, and all of us were happy.

I understood Momma's struggle to take care of us a lot better than Mark did, because Momma told me about every problem she had. I heard about late bills, the rent, the rare threat of eviction, and the constant struggle to put dinner on the table each night—things an eight-year-old just shouldn't have to worry about. But she also told me about some of the good things in her life, like how she fell in love with Daddy. She packed up and left Little Rock, Arkansas to move to New Orleans with Daddy because she loved him so much. They were young adults in love, following the beat of their own hearts.

It didn't last, though. As it turns out, the real reason Daddy moved to New Orleans from Little Rock was to be with this other woman; not Momma. He ended up leaving us when I was four so that he could start a family with her. According to him, that's why he wasn't able to help Momma with Christmas or the bills. I will honestly say that I was as stunned and hurt as Momma was when I learned that, and to this day, it's still hard to fully accept what he did to us.

But by the grace of God, Momma provided for Mark and me. Her main concern, above everything else, was keeping food on the table and a roof over our heads. She saw to it that I took care of Mark while she worked her two jobs. Until he was old enough to take care of himself, I watched over him, kept him fed, bathed him and put him to sleep every day by myself. Because I knew how hard she struggled, I made a promise to myself and to Momma that I would always be there for her, because she was always there for us.

And my biggest promise of all is to get her out of the Lower 9th Ward. How, I couldn't tell you, but I am determined to succeed. It's just too dangerous for her to live there anymore. I like my neighbors, but if I can get Momma to move somewhere safer, I will. The Lower 9th Ward is one of the poorest areas in New Orleans. Everyone there looks out for themselves. To live in the Lower 9th

Ward, you have to know how the streets are run in order to survive. An average Joe couldn't just come in there; he must know someone, or have grown up there, or he would risk being robbed or even murdered.

Despite that, I wouldn't trade my childhood there for the world. I grew up there, and I've had some good times and some bad. Although I'll never forget the good times—the neighborhood block parties where all the neighbors came together to enjoy good soul food, barbeque, and Cajun cuisine, or the good soulful R&B music played by the DJ—and how can I forget the bad times? Bad times in the Lower 9th Ward often involved drug dealers, users, and sporadic random acts of violence, which occasionally made it a living hell. But it's where we call home.

As I travel from work on Interstate 10 in the midst of bumper-to-bumper rush hour traffic, trying to take my mind off my hunger pangs and horniness by listening to the radio, one of my girlfriends, Christy, who has been like a sister to me since childhood, calls my mobile phone and kindly interrupts my mood. "Hey girl!" "Hey, what's going on?" I ask. "You still at work?"

"No, I'm leaving now. Trying to beat this rush hour traffic before it gets too bad," she says.

"Good luck, that's what I'm doing myself, and I'm stuck right in the middle of it." "Where?"

"On I-10, it's bumper to bumper, and it's hot as hell."

"Tell me about it, I can't wait to get home and strip, it's so damn hot."

Laughing slightly at her comment I vaguely reply, "Yeah, girl it's *so damn hot*. I'm sweating so bad, I'm drenched; feel like I just stepped out a shower. I can't wait to get home, get out of these clothes, eat something, and freshen up."

"Girl, who you telling? I was hoping to leave work around the time you did, but like always, Mr. Thompson wanted to have one of his long ass meetings."

"About what?" I ask.

"This upcoming Fourth of July festivities. Child, you know how New Orleans is all about the Fourth of July weekend," she says.

"Yeah, I know. Hell, it's one of the biggest events each year, how can you not know. I remember we sat in the meeting last year. So I'm sure he talked about the same thing."

"Yeah, he did, nothing new. Anyway, speaking of the Fourth, what are you doing? Is Momma cooking?"

"Yeah she's cooking, Mark says he will barbeque, are you stopping by?"

"Yeah, don't I always?" she says laughing.

"I don't know why I asked, I knew your greedy ass was coming by. Anything that has to do with food, you there."

"Whatever!"

"We need to stop talking about food; hell, I'm hungry," I say.

"Yeah so am I, I hate I didn't get to finish all of my lunch. I had to throw it away." "For what?" "Remember we was running late from lunch. I had to be at the meeting by two o'clock." "You should've taken it with you," I imply. "Now you know Mr. Thompson wouldn't go for that." I laugh at her comment, because she's right. Mr. Thompson doesn't allow anyone to eat or drink during his meetings.

"Anyway, I was asking about the Fourth because I spoke with the girls and we decided to go out that weekend," she says.

[14]

"That sounds good, after a day like I've had today, I don't care what we do. I just need to get out. So is Tasha really coming this time?" I ask with sarcasm, "Because last time she gave us some lame excuse and stood us up, talking about her brother stole her car."

Christy bursts out laughing, "Yeah she's coming," she says, laughing, "Kim is picking her up."

"Ok, I know how Kim is, she want fall for Tasha's bullshit like we do," I say, laughing, "but I'm looking forward to it."

"Me too," she replies.

With the intense heat and stop-and-go traffic, I'm getting a bit irritated, so I cut my conversation short with Christy, "Hey, I'm going to call you when I get home and settled in. Right now, holding this phone to my ear in this heat, is not helping me think straight."

"Bye girl, I would've thought you'd be almost home by now."

"Not yet, I'm still on I-10, and all of this stopping and going *in this heat*, is bringing out my road rage."

Beeeeeeeeep!!!

"Dumb ass, you see you can't go anywhere, why the hell you're trying to jump in front of me! About to cause a wreck, asshole!" I yell. "Let me go girl, before I kill somebody. I swear some people just shouldn't have driver's license."

"Ok," Christy laughs, "call me later, when you've cooled off."

"Ok." I don't have any other plans for the weekend, and I've heard that some of my favorite bands will be there, so I'm looking forward to it.

Christy and I met by playing hopscotch together on the playground of Carlson Elementary. She was an Army brat, and her family traveled frequently until her parents, Mr. and Mrs. Olsen, settled down and made New Orleans their home. We clicked on the spot, as comfortable together as if we'd known each other for years. That's when I learned she was an only child, and prone to act like the world revolved around her. She still thinks that way; she still has the sassy, sarcastic attitude that she had back then. But that's my girl. I still clearly remember telling her I'd be her play sister if she'd like, and she smiled gracefully and said okay. We made a pact that day to be best friends and to look out for one another. Even though we've grown up since then, we're still the best of friends.

It wasn't always easy, of course, and we had our differences. Moving to New Orleans was a major culture shock for her. Christy had never known that people lived in such poor conditions until my eleventh birthday party, when Momma invited her over to our house. The look on her face and on her parents' faces said it all. It was like they were ashamed even to be around us, and after that, Mr. and Mrs. Olsen thought it was best for Christy and me not to be friends anymore. It was as though they thought that, just because I lived in the Lower 9th Ward, I would set a bad example for their daughter. This was silly even then. Christy wasn't as sweet and innocent as her parents thought. Little did they know that most of the time, it was me who kept her in line rather than the other way around. But that was what they thought.

It hurt terribly to be rejected. I couldn't understand why Christy didn't seem to like me anymore, and I came crying to Momma for help. But Momma just shook her head and told me that if my friends couldn't accept me for who I was and how I lived, then they probably weren't really a friend to begin with. Then she told me, as I cried, "Angela, never allow anyone to make you feel ashamed of anything."

More than a year passed before Christy and I started to talk again. We were in middle school by then. I noticed that Christy often came to school sad, and one day, when she was sitting alone at lunch, I walked up to her and asked if she was okay.

We ended up talking straight through the lunch period. Her parents had been having marital problems, and Christy was afraid they were going to divorce. She was crying her eyes out as she spoke, and then, when she felt a bit better for having talked about it, she apologized for not being my friend and sister anymore.

Because she had treated me so badly, I didn't know what to say. I was shocked to get an apology at all. I supposed her behavior was due in part to what she had been going through at home. I remember thinking, just for a split second, *what do I say?*

Although I was hurt and disappointed by the way she had treated me, I put aside my frustration and told her the truth, expressing my feelings as best as I knew how. "I never stopped being your friend or sister," I said. "You were always considered my friend and sister. But friends don't hurt friends. I didn't do anything to make you be so mean to me. When you started telling everybody that I'm poor, saying that my house is raggedy and talking about me all mean, it hurt my feelings." By the time I was done, Christy and I were both crying. But by the end of lunch, we were good friends once more.

Over the next few weeks of school, Christy started acting out. I was never sure, but I guessed that what was going on at home between her parents was so stressful that it started to spill over into school hours. Suddenly, or so it seemed to me at the time, Christy started wanting to stay at my house after school. There she could escape from the tension at home, and avoid having to think about the problems that her mom and dad were having. She visited so often that it wasn't long before my neighbors knew her by name.

Mr. and Mrs. Olsen never cared for her coming to my house in the Lower 9th Ward. They thought it was an unfit place to live, and I guess it took them quite a while to realize that good people sometimes live in bad neighborhoods. But Momma welcomed Christy with open arms and gave her as much affection as a child of her own. She knew something wasn't right in Christy's life, but she made sure that Christy was loved and cared for anyway. Whatever stability and affection Christy was missing in her own home, she got from Momma.

I didn't mind. I had always wanted a sister to play dress-up with, since Mark wouldn't let me put him in a dress. From that point on, Christy and I were as close as any two sisters I ever knew. And fifteen years later, we still are.

#

I arrive home around five-thirty to see a few of the neighborhood kids playing in the water hydrant to stay cool. I can't help but smile, because I remember doing the same thing on hot summer days when I was a kid. Mark, Christy and I would play in the water hydrant with our neighbors' kids, having so much fun that we wouldn't stop until the fire department came out to shut the water off. Momma would watch over us, of course, while we played. She'd sit on the porch with our next door neighbor Ms. Ida Mae Williams, just talking and gossiping. They'd gossip about everything—from the pastor and his relationship with a loyal church member, to the deacon and his alcohol habit. No topic escaped their notice, especially if someone they knew was involved. And they knew everybody.

Today, however, the porch chairs are empty as I drive up. Making my way into the house, I find Momma sitting in her favorite chair in the family room, watching television and relaxing. Now, Momma is a strong stubborn woman, but I can tell this heat is beating her down and making her feel weak.

I make my way over to her and give her a kiss. "Momma," I say, placing my briefcase on the floor, "it's hot in here. Why don't you have the air on? Don't tell me you've been sitting in this house all day with no air," I add, chiding her as gently as I can.

She looks up at me with weary eyes and says, "Honey, when I was growing up we didn't have air, we had natural air. And when you get to be my age, you learn to appreciate the air God has given you." She pauses a moment, then smiles and says, "Besides, I don't know how to turn that thing on." She reaches for a newspaper instead, using it as a fan to cool herself.

I shake my head and throw a concerned frown her way, but she doesn't answer, making it quite clear that that's all she has to say on the subject.

"Where's Mark?" I ask, redirecting the conversation to cover up my frustration. If we talk about something else I'll feel better.

"Child, I don't know. I ain't seen Mark since this morning," she says. She goes back to watching television, so I walk over to the air-conditioning unit and turn it on to cool down the house.

"Why didn't Mark turn the air on when he was here?"

"I don't know, child, he just came in the house and left. You know your brother."

"Momma, you can't stay cooped up in this house when it's hot like this," I say. "You need to stay where it's cool."

"Well," Momma says, "then you need to turn the air on when you leave for work in the morning. Then maybe when you come home, I won't be sitting up in this hot house waiting for you to turn the stupid thing on." Her voice is severe, but there is humor in her eyes—classic, loving Momma.

Knowing better than to take Momma's comment to heart, I lean down to hug her, give her a kiss, and tell her that I love her. And she has the nerve to tell me, "Move, child, it's hot!" and push me gently away, laughing.

"Oh, so *now* you're hot," I say, laughing myself now. "I don't care, I'm gon' hug and kiss on you anyway, Momma."

"Get off me, child! You're making me hot."

I laugh and kiss her anyway. What can I say? That's my Momma.

Later on I prepare dinner. I decide to cook Momma's favorite meal: jambalaya with oysters instead of shrimp, and lots of spices to add an extra kick to the Cajun cuisine. I tell her all the time that she shouldn't have food with all those spices in it. The doctor has told her to cut back because of her high blood pressure. But she insists that it hasn't killed her yet, so she might as well have her favorite food the way she likes it. Now *that's* New Orleans at its finest; we have a tendency to eat everything that tastes good, but isn't necessarily good for us.

Momma comes from a long line of Creoles that originated in Cane River, Louisiana. When she was nine, her parents, Poppa Joe and Big Momma, moved to Arkansas to seek better employment and better lives for their first four children. Momma told me that she was the eighth child out of thirteen, and out of all of them, she was the only one to stay rooted in the Creole culture. Most of her siblings, including her, left Cane River to move back to Arkansas, and that's when she met Daddy. But the culture remains firmly rooted in her blood, and that cultural legacy is part of what makes Momma such a strong foundation for Mark and me. She keeps us grounded.

After I finish cooking, Momma and I sit down to eat in front of the television. One of her favorite sit-coms is on. Even though the show isn't in production anymore, she still laughs as though a new season has just begun. But tonight, through the laughter, I can tell she's worried about Mark. God only knows where he is. Mark has a tendency to come and go as he pleases, and I often tell him he shouldn't worry Momma by disappearing like he does. Although he may be over at one of his girlfriends' houses, he never calls home to let her know where he is. Tonight he isn't here, and Momma is beginning to worry. On nights like this, I will often try to keep Momma entertained until she goes to sleep so she doesn't worry. After she goes to bed, I'll get my things ready for tomorrow, take a hot bubble bath, and call it a night.

Twice a week, Momma and I spend time talking, either over lunch or just for a few hours at home. During this time, we can talk about anything under the sun. Some things I feel a bit uncomfortable talking about, because Momma can get a bit nosy sometimes when she starts prying into my personal life. It makes me nervous. She's always asking why I haven't settled down with a nice man, gotten married, and had any grandkids for her yet. She tells me all the time that if I keep hanging with single women like Christy, I will stay single. She knows Christy isn't trying to do nothing with anybody, and Momma believes I'm not trying, either.

Tonight, Momma and I talk for hours. We are so engrossed that when the breaking news report starts to play on the television in the background, I just tune it out.

"We interrupt your normal programming to bring you the latest update on Tropical Depression Steven. As of 6:15 p.m. CDT, Steven is moving northwest, traveling directly through the Bahamas toward the Florida Keys, with the potential to strengthen into a hurricane once the system has moved into the Gulf of Mexico on its way up the Gulf Coast. Doppler radar is tracking Steven's route, and

at this time our computer models predict that Steven will most likely travel along one of two distinct paths.

"One of these paths will move through the following coastal cities: Tampa, St. Petersburg, Pensacola, Fort Lauderdale, Dauphin Island, and Mobile, with the greatest impact falling somewhere between Mobile, Alabama and Biloxi, Mississippi. The other path will move through the cities of Slidell, Metairie, New Orleans, Beaumont, and Houston, with the greatest impact falling somewhere between New Orleans and Houston.

"We will continue to update you on the situation as more data becomes available. However, it is advised that everyone living within these cities should prepare to evacuate immediately to higher ground."

During our conversation, I tell Momma that I've always dreamed of getting married and having children someday. And I promise her that before she dies, I'll grant her that one wish. However, I don't think now is the right time. I'm not ready. Besides, God hasn't brought me the right man.

In her caring way, she tells me she understands, and lets me know that she doesn't want me to get into something I'm not ready for. However, she does tell me that when I'm ready, I'll know.

Uncertain, I ask, "How?"

"Well, Angela," she says, thinking carefully, "you'll know when you get that tingling feeling in your heart."

"Okay, a tingling feeling in my heart. And how will I know that?"

"When you feel it, you will know. It's a feeling that puts a smile upon your heart," she says, blushing a little.

With a gentle laugh, I remind her how, when Christy and I were teenagers, we'd sit in my bedroom planning our weddings. During that time, Christy and I were involved with two tenth grade brothers who we just *knew* we'd marry after high school. We even added their last names to our first names just to see how pretty the names would sound together.

I have to say, Mr. and Mrs. Sheldon had a cute ring to it. And we even came up with names for our kids. "Wow," I say, shaking my head at the memories, "how times have passed."

Momma looks at me with a smirk on her face and tells me she remembers those days very well. Christy and I were completely smitten over Brandon and Thomas. She says Christy and I were so infatuated with them that nobody could tell us anything we didn't want to hear. Like any high school crush, Christy and I would write 'Christy and Brandon' and 'Angela and Thomas' on just about everything we could—notebooks, papers, backpacks. You couldn't tell us we weren't in love; we wouldn't have believed you.

As Momma starts preparing for bed, the conversation continues. Momma and I start talking about leaving New Orleans. I don't know how we got to this topic, but I think we were talking about whether we would ever leave to go back to Arkansas.

"There's no way I'll leave New Orleans," I say, reaching for a comb. "Not unless I have to. New Orleans is my home and nothing can get me to leave."

Momma sits up in bed while I comb her hair for the night. "Well," she says thoughtfully, "I've been here most of my life, and there's no other place I'd rather stay other than here. Most of my brothers and sisters are still in New Orleans, with the exception of a few, so New Orleans is home. Besides, can't anything get me to leave, baby."

She thinks about it a moment longer. "Now, we may have to, but it all depends on the situation. I can definitely think of one thing that would get me up and moving. But there hasn't been anything since 1969 that has given me reason to."

I know she's thinking of the hurricane that went right past New Orleans, only a few miles away from flattening the city itself. She has told me about that year several times, saying it was the one time in her life she doesn't ever want to relive, and the scars still remain. She said that was the year New Orleans looked death in the face, and it wasn't pretty.

"But," Momma adds more cheerfully, "I've been around to see the worst of them, child, and I'm still here."

"Well, thank God," I say, laughing, "because I don't know what I'd do without you." I finish combing her hair, adding, "If something was to happen to New Orleans, God willing, we'll all still be here regardless." Momma nods, already falling asleep. Leaning over, I give her a goodnight kiss on her lips and tuck her into bed.

This is usually when I start to wind down for the night. I do my normal routine each night, which is to take a bath and then get on the telephone to talk with Christy until one of us falls asleep. Christy and I gossip about everything, from the women at work to the men they're sleeping with, and tonight is no different.

This time we talk about our love lives, and how neither of us has one. I tell her how Momma scolded me earlier about still being single. I also repeat what Momma said about why I will remain single.

Keeping it honest with Christy, I tell her, "Girl, we don't have a man because we're too picky, too busy working, or just too blind to notice him. We'll never get a man if we keep this up." I can hear the frustration in my own voice.

"Hell, I'm not picky," Christy says. "I just know what I want in a man, and I'm not going to settle for less.

If I could get the type of man I want, I wouldn't have to work with you all day."

"Yeah, okay, whatever," I reply. "But leave me out of your love life. You working all the time has nothing to do with me keeping you from getting a man. Your ass is just picky."

Hell, any man might be better than no man, I whisper to myself, fighting to stay awake. I'm not your typical night owl, though I can hang with the best of them if it means staying up with Christy and the girls. We haven't gone out together in a while. I'm really looking forward to going out with them this weekend; we've all been too busy working or furthering our education to visit much.

The girls and I would normally hang out pretty late, but this weekend we might cut the evening short and go home early after the concert's finished. Christy informs me of the weather advisory update I missed while I was talking to Momma. Because of the weather, I wouldn't want any of us to be outside getting soaked during the storm. The rain will be needed to cool things off, but the girls and I can always find some other time to catch up with each other. Besides, I'd rather be safe than sorry. You never know what could happen.

I make sure Christy knows that she can stay over at Momma's house on Saturday night if the weather forecast worsens, and I ask her to tell her parents so they won't be worried about her. It's more of a reminder than anything, because Mr. and Mrs. Olsen already know that Christy and I are inseparable. I'm sure they'd have an idea that we were together anyway. But since I know what it's like to be concerned about a missing family member—Mark still hasn't come in yet, and it's getting late—I feel it's only right to make sure they know where their daughter will be staying.

Chapter 2 He Came Out of Nowhere

*J*uly 2, 2004

*I*t's another hot day. The temperature feels like it's ninety-eight or more, and I'm sweating like crazy trying to stay cool. Christy and I are taking our lunch break at a nice café in the French Quarter. Although it's hot outside, we just have to get out of the office now and then and enjoy the ambiance, watching the people and hearing the sounds of New Orleans. So, every day, we get out among the many faces that make up our beloved city. Even watching the tourists attempting to find their way around is interesting. How some of them can end up in the middle of the housing projects Uptown is beyond me, but others manage easily enough, and most of them enjoy their vacations and have fun exploring the city's vibrant social life.

After all, what would the city be like without the tourists? A majority of the city's revenue comes from tourists visiting the casinos to gamble, or so I've read; as an administrative assistant working at the New Orleans City Hall, I hear quite a bit about the city's finances. The tourists come in, eat good food, see the sights, gamble a bit, and have a good time. Some of them, unfortunately, are later mugged or otherwise robbed of their winnings by locals trying to survive. It's a problem, but not one with an easy solution.

Trust me, if you're not working in New Orleans, you're either breaking the law or relying on government assistance. Sixty percent of the city lives below the poverty line. And seeing the tourists come into town with all of this money can tempt anyone living check-to-check or on welfare, because when you're barely making ends meet, any additional money can make a huge difference.

I have to tell you, it's bad. Better than it has been, though; there was a time when New Orleans had the number one crime rate in the United States, and things have improved a lot since then. We have a new mayor, Mayor Anthony Jones, who promises to keep the crime rate down and the local economy up. His plan is to provide jobs for communities with a high crime rate through the city's Partner for Jobs program, which requires that developers hire a certain number of unemployed citizens as a condition of being able to build here.

And we have an excellent team of New Orleans's finest law enforcers walking the beat as well. A good thing, considering that several years ago they were headline news. Not to talk badly about the New Orleans Police Department, but back then, some of them were just as crooked as the common criminals they arrested. At one point, New Orleans was nicknamed the Big Sleazy because of all the corruption.

But slowly, things changed, and for many of those who love the Bayou, a lot of those changes were good ones. There's the new Mayor; a fresh face with some interesting ideas about how to run the city. And the city government seems to be looking out for the city's interests instead of its own—at least, so far.

The café is pleasant, though, and Christy is good company, so I shake those work-related thoughts away. We aren't talking much, just enjoying the atmosphere until our orders are taken, when I look out the window and see a familiar face.

I nudge Christy, and we both look out the café window at a friend we haven't seen since college. "Is that who I think it is?" I ask, surprised.

"Is that Jamal?" she asks, staring.

"Yeah, that's Jamal! Oh my God, is he looking good!"

We become fixated as he walks gracefully through the crowd, and we find ourselves in total awe.

"*Damn*, that's one good-looking man," I say, and it's true; he's always had that athletic body, but it became especially noticeable when he was playing baseball in college. And he looks every bit of five foot ten, one hundred ninety-five pounds of pure muscle with a caramel-brown coating. "*Damn*, he's fine."

"Yeah, he is," Christy says. Jamal played baseball for South Tech as a shortstop, and he was *very* good. Last I'd heard he went on to play professional baseball in Miami, Florida. Word among fans has it that Jamal is one of the best players in the league, and I can believe it.

Caught in a daze by the aura of manliness exuded by Jamal, Christy and I stare as he continues walking down the street. Suddenly our trance is broken as the waitress cheerfully walks over.

"Are you ladies ready to order, or do you need more time?"

"No, we would like to order," I say, dragging my attention back to the matter at hand.

Christy and I place our usual orders; we both enjoy chicken and shrimp salads, and this café's salads are unusually good. I get a sweet tea and Christy is briefly undecided between getting a sweet tea or ordering a latte. The waitress takes our order and leaves, so Christy and I go back to gazing out of the window in search of Jamal. With our eyes wide open, we are keenly interested in searching for a man who is truly heaven-sent. Our search is interrupted once more as the waitress arrives with our drinks.

Christy takes a sip from her latte, then sets it down, shaking her head. "Now, *Jamal* is one good-looking man," she says, a little wistfully. "Do you think he'll remember a couple girls he said were too cute for their own good?"

"I think the man is too busy to remember anything," I reply, still watching out of the corner of my eye as Jamal fades into the distance. I imagine he's in town visiting his family. Probably doesn't have a lot of time for anything else.

It's a shame, though, because I have to admit that Jamal looks great. He's the type of man I'd love to call my own someday—hard working, good-looking, and good-hearted but with a sense of humor. The type of man I could take home to meet Momma. But who knows? Maybe God will bring someone like that my way sooner than I think.

Until then, I'll just keep praying. Even if my prayers aren't answered soon, I know they will be answered someday, if I just keep my eyes open. After all, I'm not looking for Mr. Right; I'm just looking for a man who is right for *me*. It's been a long time since I've felt real love, and the thought of raising a family with a good man is a nice one.

Waiting to receive lunch, we reminisce about college and the people we knew. Jamal was the talk of the campus. I don't know what it was about him, but whatever it was, he definitely had it going on, if you know what I mean. People just naturally liked him. He was active in sports and fairly popular.

Of course, there were other nice-looking guys on campus, but Jamal had a certain sex appeal that made many of the girls on campus—including myself—melt. Christy, on the other hand, never thought he was all that fascinating. Although she considered him an attractive guy, he just "wasn't her cup of tea." Whatever that meant, I couldn't tell you. But if that's the case, I don't think *any* man is her cup of tea.

Honestly, sometimes I wonder what she's looking for in a man. Sometimes I don't think she even knows.

If she did, I think she'd find a man quickly enough. Christy is short and petite, with a butter pecan complexion and a face that any man would yearn for. She stands an even five feet tall, and has the sexiest shape, which she knows how to flaunt to get what she needs. She is, quite simply, a beautiful woman.

But she can be incredibly hard on men. I remember, one time, she was dating this guy named Ricky. Ricky was a good-looking man who had the cutest dark brown eyes, dimples, and a smile that could really brighten up a woman's day. After two months together, she told him his conversation wasn't exciting, so she wasn't interested in dating him anymore.

Personally, I think it was just a lame excuse she used so she could exit the relationship before she got too close to him. Why, you ask? Well, just let me say I've seen her ditch guys faster than you can blink.

Trust me, she doesn't mind guys doing favors for her, but when they start doing more than she expects them to, that's Christy's cue to ditch them. In her mind, when a man does more than what's expected, the relationship is getting a little too serious. And Ricky was doing everything he could to make her happy. He would come up to the office and take us both out for lunch almost every day. He would even bring her a rose each time. He would cook dinner for her whenever he invited her over to his house, and arrange for her to get a nice massage when she was restless. She thought he was doing too much.

Granted, I can kind of see her side of it. She's looking for a partner, rather than someone to take care of her every need. But Ricky was someone I knew Christy would make a great couple with. And hell, isn't it better to have a man that does too much than to have a man who doesn't do anything at all?

The one good thing that came out of their relationship was that it raised my hopes.

Ricky had a nice job as a computer tech for a major corporation, and he had his own home, his own car, and his own bank account. When you're constantly meeting men who can't get their priorities straight, it matters a lot to know that there are some men out there who can. Even if the right one hasn't shown up yet, it helps just to know that they exist.

Finally our lunch arrives, and we indulge ourselves with a nice chicken and shrimp salad. The meal looks so appetizing. We put away our food at a leisurely pace, eating enough to get full.

But I'm still thinking about Christy and about men and relationships in general. While twirling my fork playfully in my salad, I ask, "So, when's the last time you talked to Ricky?"

Christy looks up at me, surprised. "It's been a while. Last I talked to him was about a month ago. He was closing on his new house."

"He's buying another house?" I say, amazed. I put my fork down, the food momentarily forgotten. "So where's he moving?"

"I don't know. Somewhere near the city," she says, her tone sassy.

I imagine it's somewhere close to his office, reducing the one-hour commute from his house in Lake Charles. Christy and I were invited to Ricky's house last summer for a cookout. The brother has really nice taste. The house had five spacious bedrooms, two-and-a-half bathrooms, a Jacuzzi, a two-car garage, a pool in the backyard, and a full basement. The earth-toned walls and plush carpet complemented the relaxed atmosphere of the master bedroom. The walk-in closet off the master bedroom was as big as my bedroom at home. And the bathroom off the master bedroom was just as huge, with a stand-alone shower and an adjacent whirlpool tub.

You could literally get lost just walking around the house. It was a beautiful home. He's probably the youngest person I've met with a house like that, and Christy and I were both in awe. At the time, though, she seemed more fascinated with what Ricky had and what he was doing for her than she was in the man himself, which I think is really sad. He went out of his way to please her, but in doing so, the surface was all he let her see. And in the end, she never got to know the real personality hidden underneath the roses and favors. But without knowledge of the man himself to give those favors meaning, the favors he did for her didn't matter at all.

#

During college, Christy and I played on many hearts without meaning to. We became so involved with school and work that we thought of men as a distraction, so at times men didn't matter to us. Although we went on several dates with guys who wanted a serious relationship, Christy and I never took any of them seriously. We were so focused on getting our degrees and making money that we hardly had time even for ourselves, let alone time enough to spend with a guy.

After college, Christy and I dated professional men on occasion, but we never focused on settling down with any of them. And there were some men that sent our hearts racing; heck, even one or two that we thought we could love, marry, and have a promising future with. But we were never really ready.

At least, that's what I thought until Anthony came along. He stole my heart. And looking back, I can honestly say that I wasn't ready for a relationship with him, but sometimes shit happens. We were together for a year, a long, sometimes glorious, sometimes profoundly sad year, before we broke up for good. And afterward, it took me a long while before I could even think about dating, let alone actually go out on a date.

But I learned. For one thing, the breakup made me realize that I had always taken life and love for granted. As kids, Christy and I had talked about getting married and having kids of our own as though it was destined to happen. Now that I'm older, I try to keep my hopes up, but I no longer believe that relationships are easy. And the dating scene today, God, it's like some men just don't get it. They don't seem to understand what women need.

Not that I knew what I needed either when I was younger. But at least I tried to find out. After my breakup with Anthony, I turned to Corey, a friend I'd known since high school, and the only one of my six close male friends who seemed to have a clue about women. Corey became my sounding board, my shoulder to cry on. And when I told him how frustrated I was with men, he sat down and looked me square in the eye.

"Angela," he said, "your wants and needs are two different things. Women only need five things in their life in spite of all the frivolous things they want. Those things are love, attention, time, affection, and conversation. If a man knows how to give that to his woman, his relationships might survive. You may *want* a man who would take care of you from his pocket, but what you *need* is a man who'd take care of you from his heart."

At the time, I thought Corey was crazy. He didn't even have a girlfriend, so how could he know about women? But the breakup with Anthony made me think. After I'd been grieving for a while, praying, and trying to get my life back in order, I started to see a lot of sense in what Corey had told me. Unfortunately, I haven't yet had the chance to test his advice in a real relationship, but maybe I'll be lucky soon.

"I forgot to tell you," I say to Christy, turning back to my salad. "The other night, when Momma and I were talking, she said the only thing she wanted was to see her kids have a promising future. She said her biggest wish was to see us get married and have kids of our own. And she said that life is too short, so make the best of it, but make the best of it with someone special." I hesitate, taking a sip of sweet tea to give me time to think. "I promised Momma that before she passes, I'll grant her that one wish of seeing me get married with that special someone, and I promised her she'll have grandkids one day." I turn my head to admire the scenery of the French Quarter, because it's easier than saying this to Christy while looking her in the eye. "What bothers me the most is that I'm afraid to be hurt again, you know? But I want to feel what it's like to be in love all over again with someone like Jamal or Ricky. Guys who know how to love a woman, respect her, and treat her right."

When I turn to face her again, Christy just looks back at me, stunned. I don't think I could have shocked her any more if I'd told her I was pregnant and getting married today.

"You talking about getting married?" she demands, astonished. "With who?" She reaches out to feel my forehead with the back of her hand as if testing for a fever. "Hold on now! You okay, baby? I mean, damn, what else did you and Momma talk about that got you talking like this? Are you sure that's sweet tea and not Long Island

Iced Tea?" she asks, and reaches out as if to take the tea from my hand.

I can't help but laugh. "No, it's not Long Island Iced Tea. I'm only implying that we should start taking life and love more seriously and stop playing, Christy, because tomorrow is never promised to us," I say. "Besides, we're not getting any younger." Inspired, I motion with my hand to indicate the restaurant and the street outside. "Look around, Christy. Look at all the couples here on vacation. Don't you want to feel that?" I say, gazing out into the crowd. Even from the café window, I can see couples laughing together, smiling together, taking pictures together, and even admiring the French Quarter's architecture together.

"Maybe," Christy says, sounding skeptical. "But not just yet. I'm too young to fall in love, girl. Besides," she adds, smiling wickedly, "I love being single. Can't no man do me like I do myself?"

"Yeah, and we know how you do you, frequently and often every other night!" I reply, laughing.

"That's right, and I do it damn well," she says, making a subtle gesture with her index finger.

With a smirk on my face, I reply, "You are so nasty! Get your mind out of the gutter! What I was talking about was how you do what you do with men. Every other day it's a different one who you string along. *That's* why your butt can't get one right now, because of what you do."

"Maybe I'm not trying to get one and be all faithful and committed to him yet," Christy says. "If they have a problem with me not being faithful to them, they shouldn't talk to me at all. Besides, they know we're not exclusive."

I sigh. "But there's a few that want to be exclusive, faithful, and committed. Maybe if we learned how to be faithful to ourselves, maybe we could find a man who'd be just as faithful to us." I look her in the eyes. "Besides, girl,

I've known you long enough to know that you need a man. You may not want one, but you need one."

Christy looks at me like I'm crazy. "Hey girl, nobody is complaining but you. Now," she adds, sounding a bit pushy, "get your butt up so we can get back to work before you make us late, talking all this mess."

I let the subject drop. Maybe Christy isn't ready for a relationship yet, but I think over the past few years, I've grown to understand a lot more about love and life and the ways the two coincide. Mentally and spiritually, I think I'm ready to settle down and to really feel love. And more than ever, I feel that with Momma's example guiding me, I will make a great mom to my own kids, and a good wife to some special man who loves me. Marriage wouldn't be so bad, if it meant having love and companionship for the rest of my life.

By the time we've paid the bill, Christy and I are running a little late, so we decide to take a shortcut through the alley next to the café to get back to the office. On normal days, the alley is fairly well-populated—though believe me, you wouldn't want to be caught in there at night. But today, with the Fourth of July Music Festival only a day away, the city, the streets, and even the alleyways are filled with visitors. This alley is no exception.

As I head back to work, I can't help but feel a thrill of excitement. I can hardly wait for tomorrow's concert to begin.

Chapter 3 - Celebration Time

*J*uly 3, 2004

Since the Fourth of July is on a Sunday this year, the Music Festival, which is an all-day event, is being held today instead. The temperature is in the high nineties again, with potential rain and possible flooding later tonight due to Tropical Depression Steven moving up the Gulf Coast. In spite of the weather conditions, however, over two hundred thousand visitors from out of town have crowded into New Orleans, ready to have a great time and hear some amazing music.

The Music Festival, which is always held at the Mega Dome, features entertainment from some of the latest and greatest artists in rhythm and blues, from Solstice to Ms. Nichole. This year the lineup includes one of my childhood favorites, Heat Stream, along with Momentum, Angel, Brandon, New World Order and my all-time favorite, One Sound. Now, *that's* a show worth seeing, no matter what the weather.

Christy and I arrive early and park the car in a parking deck not far from the Mega Dome. We plan to meet Tasha and Kimberly soon so we'll have time to hit the town and enjoy some of the weekend festivities before the concert starts. We promise to enjoy ourselves in spite of the blistering heat and despite the possible threat of the tropical depression and all the rain it may bring.

We find each other quickly. I think we all look splendid. Tasha is essentially a bisexual princess, with all the confidence of a diva and a great sense of humor to match. Her clothes go well with her dark mahogany complexion and her hourglass figure. Kimberly, on the other hand, is just to die for. She's heterosexual with a body that is flawless in every dimension. She is five foot eight, with brown eyes, shoulder-length hair, and a pretty face. She's mixed African American and East Indian, which gives her a slightly exotic look, and her skin is a touch darker than Christy's butter pecan skin tone. When the four of us walk around together, more than a few guys turn their heads to watch.

Upon entering the Mega Dome, we carefully make our way through the jostling crowd to our seats. Christy got some great seats for us, and I'm able to see the stage very well. When I ask, she says that she ordered the tickets more than a month in advance, and was able to get the first pick of the good seats before they were sold out. The seats around us fill in as more people arrive, and we talk to pass the time, happily catching up on recent news while the sound crew goes through the pre-concert sound checks.

Looking around, it seems like every ethnicity in the United States is represented here. I've rarely seen so many diverse cultures come together at a single event. A quick glance around the partially lit arena reveals audience members from all walks of life, which is a proud testament to the skill of the R&B singers and bands chosen to play today. Whether a given crowd member is white, Hispanic, Puerto Rican, Indian, or Latin American, there's someone on the roster they're excited to see.

While Christy and I patiently wait in our seats for the show to begin, Kimberly and Tasha decide to head to the nearby concession stand to purchase refreshments for us. Christy and I stay behind, chatting for well over fifteen minutes about everything from the upcoming show, to the latest album we've listened to, to how excited we are to see One Sound.

After considerably more than the standard "few minutes," Kim and Tasha return. They have more than just fountain drinks with them, and are accompanied by two very good-looking men, dressed in what looks like their finest attire. The two brothers, both thirty-something with light complexions, seem to have more than just the festival on their minds.

Kimberly makes the introductions. "Angie, Christy, this is Al and Robert," she says, and the two men smile in turn. "They're from Chicago. They're here in New Orleans for the weekend and looking to have a good time," she finishes, grinning.

Knowing Kimberly and Tasha, I figure two good-looking men looking to be entertained for the evening were right up their alley. Honestly, I shouldn't be surprised that they found two interested guys this quickly. But Kimberly and Tasha never cease to amaze me when it comes to meeting men. Christy and I think they play off of each other's sexual preferences, you know, pretending to be lovers just to entice men who think they will get to have sex with two women at the same time, or get to watch one do the other. It's hard to know for sure, but they do manage to find guys extremely quickly, whatever their methods.

"How are you ladies doing today?" Robert asks. His smile is wide and welcoming. "I'm Robert," he adds, holding out his hand.

Looking up at him, I shake his hand. "I'm Angie. How are you doing?" I ask.

"Fine, nice to meet you." He sounds confident and self-assured.

Al, on the other hand, heads right for Christy. He sounds almost arrogant as he says, "I'm Al. So, you must be…?"

"Christy."

"Okay," he says, making himself comfortable in an empty seat nearby. "So, are you ladies ready for the show?"

"Yeah," Christy says. "We've been looking forward to this for a while."

"And we've really been looking forward to tonight," Kimberly adds enthusiastically.

"So what's going on tonight?" Robert asks.

"Well," Tasha says, "we ladies haven't been out together in a while, so tonight is ladies' night."

Al eagerly replies, "Okay, that sounds like a great idea. So, where's the fun at tonight for you ladies, if you don't mind me asking?"

Kimberly, her behavior increasingly flirtatious, smiles and replies, "We've decided to attend the after party."

"And where's that?"

"Over at Club Fritz," she says. "On Bourbon Street."

"Okay, well, we may try to get there. I mean, we're looking to have as much fun as we can this weekend before we leave. So that's something to look forward to later," Al says.

"Well, I hope you guys enjoy it here," I say. "I take it it's your first visit?"

"Yeah," Robert says. He has really nice eyes, I notice. "We've heard about the excitement of Mardi Gras and the Music Festival, and decided we had to come down to experience at least one for ourselves."

"You guys *will* have fun, trust me," I reply. "New Orleans is a great city, and we always take care of our out of town guests."

"Yeah, you guys have been pretty good to us so far," Al says, smirking. "We may just have to come back for Mardi Gras."

I can't help but laugh at that. I'm not the only one, though; Christy and Tasha are too, and even Kimberly is giggling.

"Well, Mardi Gras is an entirely different experience," Tasha says when she has recovered enough to breathe. "Y'all just want to throw some beads, so y'all can see some girl's breasts."

After a few more minutes of talking and laughing with Al and Robert, the conversation draws to a close on a good note.

"All right, ladies, it was a pleasure meeting y'all," Robert says as he stands up to leave. "Enjoy the rest of your evening, and be safe."

"Will do," I cheerfully reply, extending my hand for a farewell handshake. "It was nice meeting you guys. Try to enjoy the rest of the evening, and don't go trying to throw some beads just to see some girl's breasts," I say, shaking my finger in mock admonishment.

"Oh, we'll try not to," Al says. "And if we don't see you ladies later, hope we'll see you next year at Mardi Gras."

"Maybe you will," Kimberly says. She's gazing into Al's dark brown eyes; he's looking right back into hers.

After a moment, he drags his gaze away and waves at the rest of us. "Nice meeting you, ladies," Al says as he and Robert casually depart from our seating area. I can see Kimberly is a little disappointed to see them go. She's not the only one. It would be nice to see Robert at the after party later.

The girls and I sit back and enjoy the show. The lights go down, and a moment later the host appears onstage to start the evening. Pretty soon the whole crowd is screaming in excitement, and the girls and I are screaming at the top of our lungs right there with them. We get up from our seats and dance to the music that plays over the arena sound system. It feels so great just to let loose and let go after all the stress at work this week.

Suddenly the music stops and the lights flicker. The host walks graciously off the stage after introducing One Sound as the first performance of the evening. The entire arena is in an uproar as the band begins to play. As the introduction to "Lonely Heart" rings out, I scream so loudly that I can feel myself starting to lose my voice.

All of a sudden, the crash of cymbals echoes throughout the arena, and the sound of drums streams out over the crowd. And as the lead singer sings the first note, Christy and I scream like two teenage groupies. It's an incredible feeling.

The show progresses, with many great acts performing some of their greatest hits and some of their newest ones. If there was one act that was worth the ticket price alone, it was definitely Solstice. They're one act that's hard to follow, and I think we all grew up listening to them. It's safe to say that the girls and I loved the concert, but we enjoyed hearing Solstice even more.

Watching them perform brought back memories of how Momma would play their album all the time on the family stereo. Momma, Mark and I would sing and dance like we were stars, listening to their great music over and over again. And watching Momma and Mark dance around the family room was a party in itself. Ah, those were the good old days. Nearly everyone in the Lower 9th Ward at that time enjoyed music by bands like Solstice and other 'old school' artists. Now, the neighborhood has been overtaken by hip-hop, and the sounds of the great R&B singers and bands are starting to fade.

When the concert is over, Kimberly, Christy, Tasha and I decide to continue our evening at the French Quarter. We exit the Mega Dome slowly, along with eighty thousand other people, and make our way through the crowd to the parking lot to get my car.

Because I parked on the upper level, it takes fifteen minutes to leave the parking deck and enter traffic at the street level due to the heavy traffic. The vehicles ahead of me move at a snail's pace as we approach the street, and I admit my patience starts to wear a little thin when I get stuck behind some visitors who don't know where they're going and seem perfectly fine with sightseeing a little while they wait. When they miss a clear opening because the driver's busy looking around at nearby buildings, I almost want to scream. Only knowing that this is fairly typical for a Music Festival weekend helps me keep my cool.

And everyone else is stuck in it, too, so why complain? Instead, I carefully proceed down to Canal Street to where we can get some much-needed food at one of the nice cafés near the French Quarter. In spite of the approaching tropical depression, the city is as active as ever. We have endured a lot of weather-related danger, so I don't think anyone is thinking of leaving the city as of yet. It looks like they're having too much fun.

With the possibility of a tropical depression heading right over us, the weather looks fairly promising, with this morning's forecast predicting a sixty percent chance of rain. Already, the sky is partly cloudy, and things have cooled off some from earlier today when we first entered the Mega Dome. I must say, the temperature feels good for the first time in a long time. We roll the car windows down, and the gentle wind blowing through the car feels so good the girls and I damn near strip our tops off in order to feel the cool air blowing gently over our skin.

From the looks on the faces of the people we pass by, I don't think any of them anticipate any major storm threat. I guess everyone is busy enjoying themselves. As I'm driving, the latest weather update comes on the radio. The weatherman issues a severe warning, advising that Tropical Depression Steven is continuing to strengthen and is still moving westwards. Despite all the fun we're having, I can't help but wonder if we were wise to come out tonight in the first place. A tropical storm is no joke, and if it strengthens into a hurricane, any cool weather we get will come at the cost of property damage and flooding for whatever towns the storm ends up hitting.

On the other hand, I've been a little nervous about Tropical Depression Steven all week, probably because it is coming at me at a time when I've got a lot of stress in my life. There's work, of course, and the fact that my car stalled again last week. On top of that, Mark has disappeared again, and now I'm starting to think more and more about needing to find a great guy and maybe settle down for once. But even knowing that it's probably nothing, I can't help but feel worried. This storm has me nervous.

Well, I think, *if I can't do anything about the storm, at least I can try to find out where Mark is*. So I talk to Christy, who uses my mobile phone to text Mark's number. I don't know when he'll get back to me, but I feel better for having done something proactive about my concerns.

As we drive to Canal Street from the Mega Dome a little rain starts to fall, which is just enough to wet the pavement. The girls and I don't mind the rain at all, so we just keep driving, moving with the flow of traffic to our destination.

Finally we make our way to the café on Canal Street. The place is jammed when we arrive. This restaurant hardly ever sees a crowd like this, except during Mardi Gras, and then it's usually packed to capacity and you need a reservation unless you want to wait for two or three hours.

Today, we get lucky and are seated after only a short wait. The smooth jazz in the background calms my nerves and lends a soothing ambiance to the dining room. I can hear relaxed voices as the café's patrons enjoy conversation with one another. The dining room is relatively quiet, and it is easy for Kimberly, Christy, Tasha, and I to talk to one another without having to strain to hear. The music blends majestically with the ever-present aroma of the Cajun cuisine that's typical New Orleans fare.

As we're waiting for our food, Mark sends a text in reply. He says he is staying at Dad's house tonight. *Well,* I think, *at least that mystery is solved.* Momma will be glad to know that her son is all right.

A few minutes later, I glance out the café window and notice paper debris flying all over the street. From the looks of it, Tropical Depression Steven is fast approaching, and the foot traffic outside has thinned. In spite of the weather, everyone continues to enjoy themselves, eating, drinking and talking seemingly without a care in the world.

I turn back to our conversation, but it seems like only four or five minutes have gone by when one of my fellow customers stands up next to the muted television hanging on the wall and says, loudly enough to get my attention, "Hey! Guys, I think you need to see this."

A silence falls over the café. One of the café employees fumbles with a remote control for a moment and turns the volume up. All eyes and ears are tuned into the weather advisory update that the National Hurricane Center has prepared.

"This is a very important weather advisory," the weatherman begins. *"The National Hurricane Center has issued a mandatory weather advisory to the following*

coastal cities: Tampa, St. Petersburg, Pensacola, Mobile, New Orleans, Beaumont, and Houston. These cities are advised to evacuate immediately.

"Over this past week, Tropical Depression Stephen has continued to move westward toward the Gulf Coast. According to the most recent update we've received, as of 6:25 p.m. Central Daylight Time, Tropical Depression Steven has intensified into a Category Five hurricane with a maximum sustained wind speed above 160 miles per hour and wind gust of 195 miles per hour. It is moving rapidly up the Gulf Coast and its diameter is getting bigger. Be advised, current estimates predict that the eye of the storm will make landfall directly over the city of New Orleans around 9:30 p.m., with the outer bands reaching the city and the surrounding region around 9 o'clock. Wind gusts will be severe and airborne debris will be dangerous. In addition, there is a strong possibility of tornadoes and a likelihood of torrential flooding in low-lying areas. A flood warning has been issued for the city of New Orleans.

"Please understand that when the eye of Steven hits, this will not mean the storm is over. I repeat, when the eye of Steven passes over the city of New Orleans, this does not mean the storm is over. Please understand that at the moment the eye passes over, it will appear that the storm has stopped, but be advised, it hasn't. The sudden calm will end and the storm will pick back up in full force. So if the eye passes over you, stay where you are. This is a very dangerous storm approaching, so please, if you are watching this and you haven't already evacuated, please do so now."

By the time the announcer has finished, some visitors have already started to leave the café for their cars or hotels. I can hear urgent voices as a few people make last-minute flight arrangements over their mobile phones, attempting to leave the city before the weather is too dangerous for the planes to leave. Others, including the family at the table immediately behind ours, launch into discussions of whether they should stay at home or leave the city, and if they were to decide to leave, where they should go.

I sit there, feeling a little numb, my eyes focused on the Doppler radar imagery of Steven grinding its way toward the Gulf of Mexico. I realize now that the storm must have gotten much worse while we were in the Mega Dome, but since the only news I'd heard since this morning was the thirty-second announcement over the car radio, I had no way of knowing how bad things really were.

I look worriedly at Christy, who looks back at me. Like the family behind us, I, too, wonder whether it is wise to remain in New Orleans. I only hope we can stay safe and dry in Momma's house while the storm rages. But even if we did decide to leave, we wouldn't have anywhere to go.

Chapter 4 – Run For Cover

*J*uly 3, 2004

*W*ith the day coming to an end, the rain finally falls at a steady pace, and I can hear the wind gusting against the window of the café. The news dictates a somber feeling, but the change of pace is welcome. Even though the weather has been menacing, we needed the rain ever so much.

By the time we've finished our martinis, half of the patrons have already left for fear of being caught out in the storm. We declare an end to the evening and depart the café. With newspapers clapped on top of our heads to keep them from getting drenched, we head out into the rain, hoping to make it home before the hurricane makes landfall. And it isn't the time to look cute anymore, so I take off my shoes and run. Thank God I parked directly across the street in front of the café, so we don't get as wet as we could've, but we get wet enough.

Dripping from the rain, the girls and I jump into my car. "Oh, my hair," I say, laughing as the water runs down my face.

"Oh, my new shoes," Kimberly replies, and we all take a moment to laugh. "Oh my God, it is pouring down," says Tasha. "We need to take our butts home right now," Christy says, "because this rain is coming down hard. Ya'll heard the weatherman, you seen all of those people leaving. That's why we're leaving too."

"Look at us, we're soak and wet," I say.

"I'm not going anywhere like this," Tasha makes known. "Hell, I don't think any of us will be going anywhere in all this rain," says Christy, "take us back to the car so we can go home." "Yeah, I just ruined a brand new pair of shoes," Kimberly rants.

"You're worried about some damn shoes that you'll wear only once. You need to be worrying about getting out of this rain and getting your butt home safe," I say.

"Whatever, the sooner you get us to my car, the sooner we can get home," she says. Raining cats and dogs, my windshield wipers are struggling to keep up. I can barely see. Driving ever so slowly down Royal Street, I take Kimberly back to her car near the Mega Dome so that she and Tasha can get home safely. Creeping through the narrow streets, past tourists running to get out of the rain, we quickly meet the madness of gridlock traffic.

I turn on the radio so I won't miss anything important. The weatherman on the news there repeats that Hurricane Steven is approaching and everyone needs to take precautions. Coming in from the Gulf of Mexico with a maximum wind speed near 157 mph, it's moving at a much faster pace than the National Hurricane Center expected, and with a much higher potential for causing damage. The weatherman also reminds us that Hurricane Steven will hit New Orleans with deadly force between 9 p.m. and 9:30 p.m. tonight, and they're advising the entire city to evacuate immediately.

According to the weatherman, when Steven makes landfall it will make a direct hit on New Orleans as a

[49]

possible Category Five, which is the most powerful type of hurricane, packing winds of 156 mph or more. That type of maximum wind speed could level my beloved hometown, turning thousands of people into refugees. And the 100-year-old prediction of the Doomsday storm is looking ever more possible. Right now we're feeling the force of the outer band of Hurricane Steven. Looking out the side windows once more, I can see trees swaying and the rain dancing. The rain is now coming down in sheets, and the wind is blowing more wildly and violently. Already, it appears that the drainage system is having difficulties keeping up with the massive overflow of rain.

Like many residents who call New Orleans home, Christy and I won't evacuate the city. Besides, how would we leave? Every plane and train leaving is booked. And Momma isn't getting on anybody's airplane, even if we could find a seat. And my car stalls on a regular basis, so we won't make it to Arkansas. I tell myself not to worry. We've been down this road before and have managed to ride out storms like Hurricane Mitch and Beth, which struck with almost the same intensity as Steven might. So we really don't have any choice but to stay and ride this one out as well, hoping Steven won't be worse than any other storm that has hit New Orleans, as the National Hurricane Center anticipates.

Governor Ashley Brown finally declares a state of emergency, asking everyone in New Orleans and the surrounding parishes to evacuate immediately for higher ground. In a sudden frantic move, Mayor Anthony Jones quickly issues his own mandatory evacuation, insisting that everyone leave the city and get the hell out. "This will be the worst storm we've ever seen," he says. "Worst case scenario, traffic on Interstate 10 stalls and comes to a standstill with nowhere to go. That is my fear," he says, sounding worried. "Everyone in low-lying areas must leave right now or look death in its eyes."

This is even more serious than I thought, I think, as I hear those words on the radio. *I just hope Christy and I can make it home in time.*

With so many people in town for the weekend, everything becomes chaotic. Many tourists are racing to the airport and train station in hopes of catching the last flight or train out of the city before those are all cancelled and they're stuck. Fearing the gas stations might run out of gas, others rush to fill up their cars with gas before they leave. It's pure pandemonium.

Where they're going, no one knows but them. But I'm sure it's miles away from New Orleans. Half of the evacuees are tourists who came to New Orleans to enjoy the city and have a great Fourth of July weekend. The other half are residents of New Orleans who can afford to leave. The rest of us are left alone to pray for our safety.

Driving home, traffic comes to an abrupt halt. Cars stalled miles and miles ahead of me creep westbound on Interstate 10, searching for higher ground. Most of the evacuees are hoping they will not be caught on the highway when Steven hits. But it's becoming apparent that they might be. Traffic is moving at a sluggish pace. And just judging by the looks on their faces it's obvious the drivers around me are getting just as irritated as I am from sitting on this jammed highway, because the angry sounds of their car horns can be heard all over.

With nowhere to go in either the east- or westbound directions, everyone is at a standstill, waiting for a break in the traffic and hoping not to run out of gas. The rain and thunder are so frightening that I just wish the storm would hurry up and end. I wish I hadn't driven home this way when I could've taken Claiborne all the way home. I' thought maybe traffic wouldn't be so bad going this way, but I guess I was wrong.

The rain falls constantly as we move ever so slowly forward. And the sustained wind from Steven is blowing heavily. Frustrated with the stop-and-go traffic, I pick up my mobile phone to call Momma.

"Hey, Momma," I say.

"Hey, where ya'll at?" Momma asks.

Trying not to lose my cool, I reply, "Christy and I are on our way home. We're stuck in traffic," I say, keeping my composure. "Do you need anything?"

"Yeah," she yells, "for you and Christy to get home and get out of this rain. I don't know why you girls are out there in this stuff anyway. It's a hurricane out there! Ya'll need to get on here," Momma says, fearful and concerned.

"Okay, Momma, we are, and make sure you turn off that TV," I say.

"I'll turn it off when I finish watching *Good Gracious*. Now you girls get home!" she demands. I can tell by the tone of her voice that she's worried.

"Okay, Momma, we're on our way! Love you, kiss, kiss," I say, laughing my way off the phone. Christy laughs, too.

"Momma is a mess. Let's get home before she kills us both," she says. "While I'm at it, let me call home and let my momma and daddy know that we're okay, and we're getting out of this mess and going to your house. I'm sure they're worried about us, too."

Trying not to get irritated with the traffic, my patience starts to run short. I have to say, I've never been in anything like this, and it has gotten aggravating. A news flash of a shortage of gas is announced over the radio. That worries me. I only put enough gas in the car to get us to and from the Mega Dome.

Like everyone else, Christy and I have now been sitting in this traffic jam for nearly an hour. And from the look of my gas meter, I don't know if we will even make it to our exit if we continue at this pace.

The gray cloud cover has made it significantly darker. We have only one exit to go, and it feels like a country mile, as visibility is limited. The rain has let up slightly, though not enough for me to turn off the windshield wipers, but the wind continues to blow ferociously and the thunder continues to rumble.

The latest weather report had Steven bearing down on the Gulf Coast as a Category Three hurricane. No one was sure of the accuracy of its direction, but it had already made landfall over the Florida Keys. A forecast prediction had Steven hitting New Orleans as a Category Five hurricane, but meteorologists were unsure of his projected path, whether he would go toward Texas or hit New Orleans straight on as they'd first thought. However, once Steven crossed over the warm waters of the Gulf of Mexico, he regained strength. So now we're just waiting for his grand entrance. From the look of the heavy wind, rain, thunder, and lighting, Steven appears to be coming ashore within minutes. Earlier in the week, Steven was just a tropical depression surging out in the Atlantic, then within hours he became a tropical storm headed for the Bahamas. Now he's becoming a full-blown threat that is hard to monitor accurately because of constant changes in his progression.

Finally we move at a snail's pace to our exit. Hundreds of cars are backed up on the entrance of Interstate 10, headed east in an attempt to leave the city. I think Christy and I are the only two going in the opposite direction, away from the traffic leaving New Orleans.

Approaching the intersection, a well-groomed New Orleans police officer who appears to be in his late thirties screams out over the rumbling thunder while monitoring traffic. "All traffic is being diverted onto the highway, moving eastbound away from the coast!" He has to scream to be heard amidst the pouring rain.

"Any cars going to the Lower 9th Ward, Jefferson, and St. Bernard Parish must turn around immediately or be forced to evacuate!" The officer is yelling with frustration in his voice. Just by the look on his face and the tone in his voice, it's obvious he's concerned about his family's well-being, because the weather is getting worse.

With a very irritated look I yell back, "I'm going home to get my momma and brother!" I know damn well this old car of mine couldn't travel eighty miles without overheating and stalling.

"Okay," he shouts over the pounding rain, "but you girls need to get your family and your things and get out of here before the storm comes, you hear?" Even while he yells, he continues to direct traffic in an orderly fashion and at a steady pace.

"Yes, sir!" I answer at the top of my voice.

With no intention of coming back to the highway to evacuate, we drive down N. Claiborne Avenue to get home before the storm strikes. For miles, headlights are all we can see, from motorists leaving in a last-minute effort to evacuate. It's a sight to see so many cars getting on the highway at one time. The way things are looking, I'm not sure they'll make it out before Steven makes landfall. If they don't, many lives may perish on Interstate 10.

Driving several miles down N. Claiborne, we hit a sudden traffic jam. Louisiana State Troopers dressed in yellow reflective raincoats are directing hundreds of evacuees to Interstate 10. All lanes of N. Claiborne have been diverted to go only one direction—except the far right lane going down N. Claiborne. As it appears that Christy and I are the only ones going the wrong way, it's like weaving in and out of one-way traffic.

As we reach a stopping point, we're approached by a nearby state trooper who appears to be just as anxious as I am to get out of this mess. As the rain pours down, beating against my window, I'm hesitant to roll it down to acknowledge him for fear of getting drenched. The rain has started coming down heavily again. The seconds are ticking down like a timer on a bomb. It looks like any second now Steven's going to come roaring over the horizon.

The trooper has a keen awareness of the weather, and it doesn't appear like he's in the mood for any hesitation from me or from anyone. Hurrying up traffic so he can get out of the storm and to his family, he yells, "You can't go down that way! All traffic going to the Lower 9th Ward is being diverted back to the Interstate. It is advised that you evacuate the city immediately."

"I know!" I scream. "I'm going home!" I reiterate to the trooper over the sound of thunder, "I was told by the New Orleans police officer at the Interstate I could go home to get my momma and brother."

"Okay, but you need to hurry up and do just that, and make it back in the next half hour before we shut this exit down!" he orders, while still using his flashlight to signal traffic to move. "Keep it moving, let's go, people, keep it moving!" he yells to the traffic. He looks at me again. "After the roads are closed, no one will be allowed on these streets except law enforcement," he says while directing me to an open lane. "This is the only lane going to the Lower 9th Ward! Take this lane home, get your mother and brother, and get back up here as soon as possible! This lane will close down in about twenty minutes to allow all traffic to leave the Lower 9th Ward and St. Bernard Parish," he says firmly.

"Okay!" I yell. "Thank you."

Looking at the clock on the dashboard of my car, I see it's now 8:24 p.m., and Christy and I aren't anywhere near home. In these turbulent weather conditions, it's going to take fifteen minutes, maybe more, just to get down N. Claiborne to home. And the weather is getting worse. To stay updated, we listen to the local radio station, where it has been announced that Steven's outer bands have overtaken the entire state of Louisiana and have spun off several tornadoes within the surrounding areas of Shreveport, Baton Rouge, Lafayette, and Alexandria. Debris is flying everywhere. We need to hurry up and get home.

Chapter 5 - Suddenly, It Happened

*A*rriving home just in the nick of time, Christy and I park the car with little time to spare. I have to tell you, I've never been in a storm like this before. I thought Hurricane Mitch was bad, but Steven has come and proven different. It's much bigger, much more powerful, and far deadlier.

With the wind blowing so hard, we barely make it out of the car. Fighting the severe wind gusts and torrential rain, we're darn near swept off our feet and plunged onto the driveway, which is now flooded with rain. Soak and wet, we finally make it inside.

"Momma, we're home!" I yell. My voice echoes through the small bungalow house I've lived in for twenty-seven years.

Momma yells back from the family room in the middle of the house, "'Bout time! What took you girls so long? You called over an hour ago. It doesn't take that long to get here."

Kicking off soaked and wet shoes, Christy and I walk toward the family room.

"Hey Momma," Christy says, walking over to give her a hug and kiss.

"Hey baby, I'm gon' beat both of ya'll," Momma says. "You girls shouldn't have been out in this mess anyway, trying to go to some dumb show when there's a hurricane out there. And look at you and Angela! Soakin' wet," she says, shaking her head at us. "Go get outta them clothes," she says, agitated.

Walking over to give Momma a kiss as she sits in her favorite chair, Christy goes to stand near the fireplace.

"Just be glad we made it home safe, Momma," I tell her as I kiss her on the lips. "Besides, traffic was bad."

"Get off me with them wet clothes," Momma insists.

"I am," I say, laughing. "Can I kiss you?"

"When you get out them wet clothes you can," she says angrily.

I kiss her one more time on the cheek as water drips from my soaked hair. Momma nudges me slightly.

"Move now," she says, a look of annoyance upon her face. "I don't want that mess on me. Get outta here, and change clothes! Go on before you girls get sick."

"You gon' take care of us," I say.

"No, I'm not! I'm not taken care of ya'll grown butts!" she says, "If you and Christy would've gotten here when you said you were on the way, you wouldn't have gotten all wet."

"Traffic was bad," I say.

"Yeah and so is the weather, but that didn't stop ya'll from going to some dumb show when there's a hurricane out there!" she yells brashly. "That's why ya'll wet."

Laughing, Christy asks Momma, "Was you worried?" and like any parent who loves their kids, Momma replies, "Of course!"

Taking Momma's advice, Christy and I walk into my bedroom to change clothes before we catch a cold and get sick.

As Christy enters my bedroom, Momma asks, "Christy, did you call your momma and daddy to let them know you are over here and okay?"

"Yes, I called them earlier," she says. "They know I'm here, Momma."

"Okay."

In my room, Christy and I change into something warmer and more comfortable and then make our way into the family room, where we sit nervously waiting for Steven's arrival. Momma made hot tea for us while we were changing.

Suddenly, the wind and the rain intensify with unimaginable force. I think of the trooper directing traffic. Christy and I made it inside, but the trooper must still be out there, knowing every minute he stays to direct traffic might help a few more families get to safety. I hope he is able to rejoin his own family soon.

We stay updated on the latest conditions by watching the Weather Channel. The National Hurricane Center advises us that Steven will be the first hurricane in decades to make a direct hit on New Orleans. And the damage and death toll could be catastrophic.

At 8:55 p.m., we are informed that the eye of Hurricane Steven is nearing New Orleans, with sustained winds now blowing at one hundred and forty-eight miles per hour. News has circulated that the wind gust and rainfall from Steven's outer bands have toppled electrical lines, knocking out power in some neighborhoods, while heavy rainfall is reported to have flooded the streets in some parts of the city. And in some places, the wind has caused major structural damage to buildings. Fortunately, we still have electricity in the house.

I guess my one reason to leave New Orleans is really coming. But it's too late to leave now. Besides, I don't even trust that my car would have made it to higher ground. The car stalls on a regular basis, so I only trust it to go as far as the vicinity of New Orleans itself.

"Well, Momma," I say, giving voice to my thoughts, "I suppose this gives us our reason to have left New Orleans."

"I suppose," Momma says. "But I wasn't going nowhere. I told you already, I've seen the worst hurricanes to hit New Orleans, and I haven't left yet. So I wasn't leaving, no matter how bad it got."

"Yes you were," I say. "Christy and I would've made you. Besides, you haven't seen a hurricane like *this*. They say this one is far worse than any storm to ever hit New Orleans before. So I think we should've left, somehow. We said we'd leave if it got catastrophic. And the weatherman said it has," I say. "So I think we should've left temporarily, just to be on the safe side, if only for a brief moment. I believe we could've left and came back in a day or two to see how bad it was because the weather's really getting bad out there."

Momma frowns at me. "Well, it's too late to leave now. Besides, where were we going? We don't have any money to stay in a hotel or catch a train, and you know your old raggedy car won't make it up the street," Momma says. "It's going to pass over like they all do. And when tomorrow come, we'll wake up to see how bad it was, like we always do." She straightens. "So, you and Christy go get the emergency kit from the kitchen so we'll have something to eat and drink for a few days," Momma says. "Everything should still be good. You may have to add a few things."

More than an hour later, after bringing out the emergency kit and telling Momma about the concert we went to, the three of us go to the family room to listen to the news and hopefully learn more about the weather outside. Listening closely to the Weather Channel, I quickly become more aware of the potential danger.

"Good evening. I'm Cindy Evers, reporting live from stormy New Orleans, which is now taking a beating from the rain and wind. As you can see, the wind is now blowing extremely heavily, and the rain is coming down in buckets." She screams in order to be heard over the wind and storm, all the while fighting to keep her balance as she is pushed by the relentless rain and wind. *"Looking around, I can see debris flying everywhere. Palm trees are bending like they're made of rubber."* I can tell it's bad just by watching her fight the wind in an effort to remain stable and not get blown away.

"Wow, look at that," I say.

With our eyes glued to the television, we're all in awe over what we're seeing.

"I can't believe this," Christy says, shocked. "We were just out there. We were just driving right in the area she's at! Oh my God."

"Well, I'm just glad ya'll made it home," Momma says. "I was concerned about ya'll. That's why I was calling, to tell you and Christy to hurry home."

"Well, we made it, Momma," I say.

"Barely," Christy says. "We just drove through the city a few hours ago. Now look at it. That lady's out there darn near getting blown away. That could've been us!" Christy says, clearly frightened. "And we had the nerve to make plans to go to Fritz for an after party. Are we crazy?"

"Yeah," Momma says. "Just like that lady, out in this mess reporting the weather. She's crazy for being out there."

Christy and I both smile. "She's not crazy, Momma." I say. "She's just doing her job. And we're not crazy, either. We came home as fast as we could."

"Yes, you are," Momma retorts. "You were out there, thinking 'bout going to some crazy party. Ain't nobody going to no party in this mess, and if they are, they're just as crazy as you and that weather lady."

Laughing, now, Christy sits down on the sofa. Some of her fright seems to have passed. "She's *not* crazy, Momma, she's just doing her job," she reiterates.

Momma shakes her head. "Well, if that's her job, then she needs to get a new one, because anyone doing a job outside in a hurricane has to be crazy."

I have to tell you, Momma is a mess. She says the darndest things sometimes. But I have to agree, I sure wouldn't want to have a job that made me go outside in weather like this.

Tuned in to the television, we fall silent as we listen closely to Cindy give her report. In the background I can clearly hear the wind blowing fiercely against the house, a noise like a loud whistling sound. *"The outer band of Steven has now come ashore, but the intensity of the storm isn't as severe as it will be once the strongest part of Steven arrives in New Orleans with brute force winds. Keep in mind that this is a dangerous system. With the exception of a few New Orleans police squad cars patrolling the city, you can see the entire city is now empty."* She yells her words over the hurricane-force wind while pointing at a police car driving in the background.

It's amazing to think that within the past several hours, the city was filled with vacationers from all over the world who'd come here to celebrate the holiday weekend. I see they have taken heed to the warnings and have long since gone.

"The National Weather Service says Steven will make landfall in New Orleans around 9:35 p.m. as a Category Five hurricane. And as the storm hits New Orleans, projected winds will reach 160 miles per hour," she screams. *"Due to extreme warm conditions and sea surface temperatures in the Gulf of Mexico, Steven has unexpectedly strengthened. This storm has become a monster headed directly for New Orleans. And the wind alone will cause massive property damage. However, the storm surge will be just as catastrophic, reaching anywhere between ten and twenty feet. This will truly be the storm of our century. It is massive in size and barreling down at tremendous speeds, so everyone in the path of the storm needs to take shelter. Even if you think you can ride this one out, please take shelter* immediately, *because this one is going to be bad,* really *bad. This is Cindy Evers with the Weather Channel, reporting live from New Orleans."*

With the threat of Steven approaching, Christy and I gather some extra food and water to add to the emergency kit Momma prepared during last year's hurricane season. With batteries, flashlights, a radio and a first aid kit assembled, it should help to carry us through for several days after the storm passes, which I believe should be enough to last us until emergency aid arrives.

Suddenly, the lights flicker. Through the window, I watch as lighting illuminates the sky. Thunder rumbles aggressively, and the force of it makes the old bungalow tremble. Grabbing the flashlights, Christy and I walk back into the family room, leaving the emergency kit on the kitchen counter near the refrigerator.

The steady downpour of rain has become a huge concern, with major flooding becoming all too possible. And with a potential storm surge of ten to twenty feet, some structural damage is expected. I wonder if New Orleans's levee system is built to withstand that much water, let alone the additional force from a Category Five hurricane. So the thought of seeing my neighborhood destroyed has become a constant worry. And the Industrial Canal isn't too far from the Lower 9th Ward, so if the levees do breach, we're facing a major problem.

With all eyes on the television, we sit in the family room, watching the Weather Channel for updates. Neither Christy nor I utter a word. Momma sits in her favorite chair while Christy and I sit nearby on the couch adjacent to the hallway. I notice Momma constantly glancing over at Mark's high school prom picture, which sits on the mantelpiece over the fireplace. I can tell Momma's concerned about Mark's whereabouts. Not wanting to see her worry needlessly at such a detrimental time, I tell her that Mark texted me on my mobile phone earlier today. "He's okay," I reassure her. "He's over at Dad's house."

"Oh God, thank you," she says, obviously relieved. "I was just sitting here thinking about that boy of mine." She glances at the television with great concern in her expression. "Why didn't he just pick up the phone and call me, let me know something? I haven't heard from him in two days."

Walking over to comfort her, I give her a huge hug and a kiss on the forehead. Then I gently remind her, "Now, you know Mark isn't gonna call you from Dad's house, Momma. Since Dad's been gone, Mark doesn't want to start no mess with you about Dad. He knows you're still angry with Dad for leaving us. So why would he call you from there?"

"Well, I don't care where he calls from."

"Yes, you do. If you didn't, you wouldn't be worried," I say.

Momma looks perturbed. "He could've called from the moon, as long as he called me."

Suddenly a huge gust of wind slams into the house. I hear a massive tearing noise.

"Oh my God," Momma says fearfully. "What was that?"

"Sounds like the roof," I say, guessing. If it were one of the walls, the noise would have been even louder.

"The wind is blowing the shingles off the roof, Momma," Christy says, agreeing with me.

With one last flicker, the electricity finally goes off. Quickly, I grab a flashlight so we can see.

"Momma, you okay?" I ask.

"Yeah," she replies tersely. "I just can't see."

"Just hold on, Momma, let me turn on the other flashlight," Christy says.

Now, with both flashlights on, we make our way from the family room and into the hallway leading to the kitchen. It's our safe haven, one of the best-protected places in the house.

"We could stay in the hallway to help cut down on the wind," I say. My voice is higher than usual. I feel a little panicky, after all that I've seen on the Weather Channel about possible flooding and storm damage.

"Come on, Momma, let me help you," Christy says, taking Momma gently by the arm. "We have to get into the hallway before the wind picks up any."

In fear for our lives, we race into the hallway. The wind slams into the house again, this time causing the front entrance to collapse. Water starts to rush in. Hurricane Steven has now made landfall. Frightened by the storm, we gather together to help shield one another against the wind. The water ever-so-slowly begins to rise. Within minutes, it's up to our knees.

"We have to get to the attic," I say, breathing heavily. "If the water keeps rising like this, we'll all drown."

I can see the fear of death on Momma's face as she gasps for air. The pressure from the wind is strong enough to knock the wind out of you, and it's hard to breathe normally.

"I'm tired," she says. "I can't make it to the attic."

"Come on, Momma!" Christy sounds frantic as she yells over the wind. "We have to get to the attic before the water gets any higher! I can't swim, so we can't stay down here!"

The roaring wind sounds like a freight train as the three of us move carefully down the hallway. With the water now waist-high and rising, I pull the ladder down from the hallway ceiling. My grip on the flashlight slips, and I accidentally drop my flashlight into the water, where it dies instantly. Hoping the water doesn't rise any higher, we climb into the attic for relief. Although it is drier here, I still feel afraid. If the water does rise into the attic, we will be forced to make it to the rooftop somehow for safety. If we can't and the water traps us here, we're all going to die.

The few minutes in the attic feel like hours as the storm batters the roof above us. It's extremely hot up here, and damp. And the wind seems even stronger as it bangs up against the house, shaking it all the way down to its foundation, while we sit in the attic and pray for the storm to hurry past. It feels like God Himself is shaking the earth, and the noise is a horrifying rumble, worse than anything I've ever heard. If this is what an earthquake feels like, my God, I *don't* want to be in one.

As the outer bands rage over the Lower 9th Ward, I can only imagine the powerful winds causing incredible destruction, ripping houses from their foundations and tossing them around like dollhouses.

The three of us find ourselves holding on for dear life to a wooden beam in the attic. It supports us, keeps us close together, and helps us to hold out against the wind. But the rain continues to pour down, heavier and heavier, and now I can feel water rising to touch the bottoms of my feet. Floodwaters have almost risen into the attic. The wrath of Steven is being felt across the city, as the nonstop wind and the torrential rain batter my neighborhood. The wind is so strong now we can barely catch our breaths. Every gust of wind makes it all but unbearable as we struggle to hold on.

With tears in her eyes, Momma prays vigorously. "Heavenly Father, Who watches over us in the midst of the storm, keep us safe and sound. Continue to comfort us and lead us from harm's way. Amen," she finishes. Her plea is heartfelt.

"Amen," Christy and I say.

Struggling to brace ourselves against the torrential rain and gusting wind that is shaking the entire house, I interlock my hands around Momma's waist to help hold her up as we brace against the wooden beam. "Hold on, Momma! I got you! I won't let you go!" I yell.

"Hold on Momma, we got you." Christy has to shout over the roar of thunder. She, too, is holding onto Momma for dear life. "We got you!"

With the wind and water beating on us, Momma becomes even wearier. Her hands get tired of holding onto the wooden beam, and I can feel her hold grow weaker. "I'm tired. I can't hold on," she says. She sounds exhausted. Christy and I reach out, grabbing hold of her arms to help keep her upright.

"Hold on, Momma, just hold on. We got you," I scream.

Beside me, Christy holds on just as fiercely. "We got you, Momma, just hold on and don't let go," Christy yells. I can see tears in her eyes every time the lightning flashes.

Suddenly, the house begins to shake uncontrollably. A portion of the roof gives way, crashing down with a sound like a fallen tree.

"Ahhh!" Christy screams as water rushes in through the hole like a tidal wave. Plunged beneath the water, Christy lets go of the only flashlight we have left. I hold on to her, but the force of the storm drags her away and pulls me underwater. Our hands are forced apart, and I feel Momma's hands break free as I struggle to gain any kind of control over my footing. I reach for her in the pitch-black darkness, struggling as I battle to overcome the pouring rain and the terrible wind that has now pushed Momma out of my reach.

"Help! Help!" I hear someone screaming faintly in the distance.

"Momma!" I scream, diving in to save her. A short distance away, Christy emerges from underneath the water, gasping for air.

"Oh God," she screams, "we're gonna die!" I can only barely hear her over the wind. But there is not a shadow of a doubt in my mind. I'm *not* letting us die like this.

As I swim toward Momma, her voice begins to fade in the distance. I fight the wind and rain, making every attempt to get her, but I can't tell where she is. The lightning only lets me see in split-second flashes, and the water around me is so dark that I can't see much of anything. I can only hear the whisper of Momma's voice calling me. "Angela! Angela, help!"

In a blink of an eye, Momma is whisked away. The wind pushes her further out into the floodwaters. "No!" I scream, swimming frantically. "Momma, Momma!" In spite of the darkness and the severity of the storm, I swim out into the storm-tossed night in an effort to save her.

Determined to rescue Momma from the storm's grasp, I move toward the area of water where I last heard her cry out. But my efforts are soon overpowered by the brute force of the wind, which takes the breath out of me with every stroke I make. The rain beats upon my body like pellets. It's growing harder to breathe, and I'm running out of steam. Tonight, however, I'd rather run that risk and die than give up on trying to save Momma. In a last-ditch attempt, I try once more to find her, but the wind is so severe that I quickly find myself struggling to even move. I make every attempt to move forward, but the force of the wind is so powerful it seems to have suspended me in place. My attempts are futile.

Behind me, Christy struggles to speak as she fights for air. "Angela," she says, breathing heavily as she accidentally takes in water, "Angela, help me, I can't move my leg! The roof is on it," she cries, falling briefly silent as the rough water impairs her ability to speak.

Oh God, why me? Here I am, faced with the possibility of losing both my Momma and my best friend at the same time. The water is rising faster by the minute. Unless I turn back, my own death appears imminent, because it's fast becoming hard for me to keep my head above water. And I'm getting tired of fighting. I want to give up, to relax for the first time in hours. But I can't do that and also save someone.

With my thoughts racing, suddenly I'm paralyzed. Everything in my world comes to an abrupt halt as Momma's scream resonates throughout my head. I don't know what to do except cry. And in my ear I hear a soft whisper, as someone takes a last breath. "Angela..."

"Momma!" I scream, turning frantically in the dark to follow the voice.

"Angela," the voice says again. Moving in search of the whisper, I scream, "Momma, where are you?" Feeling my way blindly in the dark, I'm tossed here and

[69]

there like a rag doll, striking every object imaginable that is floating in the attic. "I'm over here," the voice whispers again. And with the sound of sputtering water, I hear her say, "Angie, we're gonna die. I can't feel my leg."

Suddenly, her head slips under the surface of the water.

"Christy!" I scream. Following the voice, I race over to save her. A gust of wind violently overtakes me in the total darkness and I'm pushed vigorously into a wall. "Aahhh!" I scream as I feel a sharp thump against my right arm. Moving now off of pure adrenaline, my heart is pumping ten times faster than normal as I barge over to Christy and plunge underneath the water to pull her out from underneath the fallen roof. I'm not going to let her die on me like I've just let Momma die. Holding onto each other for comfort, Christy and I sit frightened in one corner of the attic. The water has risen up to our chins. Our only hope of survival is to go out into the storm and climb atop the battered roof. With Christy's leg severely injured, we carefully attempt to maneuver together in order to combat the wind and rain. The wind is so strong we can barely hold on, but we have to get out of this attic. It's either die in it, or die trying to survive. The noise has become all but unbearable. The pressure is making my ears pop, and now that some of the adrenaline rush has ebbed, my arm is killing me.

As the wind and the rain subside a little, Christy and I finally make it atop the roof in a last frantic scramble. While the rain and wind continue to beat down on our weary bodies, we hold on for dear life to what's left of the chimney, hoping not to get blown away into the water. Exhausted, we collapse, teary-eyed, as the rain continues to pour down. Sprawled out on top of the damaged roof, Christy and I hold each other as we cry.

Then the wind dies, and I lift myself up a little, blinking. Is it over? Could this be the end of it? The storm has stopped, just like that. Taking in a deep breath, I inhale and then exhale, crying to God, "Thank you, thank you, it's over!"

I'm so tired from the struggle, I'm not sure I could have taken any more. Christy and I shift positions, holding tight to each other for dear life as we move up against the chimney. The wind is still blowing and the rain is lightly falling, but nothing like as severe as before. It's pitch black and we can't see a thing, but it's so calm and quiet. Christy and I sit, overwhelmed by the sudden silence. We don't know what to expect now that it's over. Maybe the rescue workers will come soon. Sitting in complete darkness and near-silence, we enjoy the tranquility and attempt to relax.

Within minutes, all hell breaks loose. Steven picks up momentum again, and in ten minutes, we're back where we started. It's another round of wild, torrential rain and wind battering at us like the ocean has somehow fallen from the sky. I quickly realize the eye has just passed over us, and we're about to be struck by the second half of the storm.

"Oh God, no," Christy cries out when I tell her. She sounds exhausted and terrified. "God, not again. What is happening? Please make it stop, please!"

I cling to her as she pleads to God. Sputtering to breathe now, due to the heavy wind and rainfall, we hold onto one another ever so tightly and bury our heads against each other's shoulders as if to hide from the rain and wind. I only hope it will help keep the water from blowing into our mouths. It's so cold, we're shivering. I think hypothermia is setting in.

Hoping that our dual body temperatures will keep us warmer, we snuggle up closely together as the rising waters overtake the rooftop. With the lower half of our bodies now submerged in the water, we just sit near the chimney and pray for it to end. It feels like two hours of hell as the storm crashes down upon us once again. Dimly, I think, as the evening changes into early morning, *what a way to celebrate the Fourth of July.*

Chapter 6 - Sisterly Bond

*J*uly 4, 2004

*T*he storm is finally over. Awakened by the sun's rays and the roaring sound of a helicopter flying above, Christy and I rise from where we lie on the battered rooftop that's now only partially visible in the flood, and see the entire Lower 9th Ward under water.

Badly bruised, exhausted, and sleep-deprived, I can't help but moan aloud from the excruciating pain in my arm. "Oh God," I say, holding my injured arm with my free hand to keep it from moving and hurting me even more. Struggling for purchase atop the roof, Christy clings to me, shivering from the coolness of the water.

"Christy," I grunt, "are you okay?" She nods her head slightly, but I can tell she isn't entirely responsive.

I'm worried about her condition, so I gently nudge her, calling, "Christy, Christy," in a quiet voice. I groan while adjusting my position on the roof to get more comfortable. In doing so, I accidentally place my hand upon her leg.

A second later, she buries her head in my lap and screams. Clutching onto my shirt with one hand, she reaches for her leg with the other. Her face is contorted with agony.

"Christy! Christy! Are you okay?" I ask, frightened at her sudden outburst.

For a moment, she doesn't answer, just cries softly from the pain. When she can speak again, she lifts her head and moans, "My leg, ow, my leg."

I'm not sure what the problem might be, but whatever's wrong, I just hope to God it's not broken. I'm no doctor, so I can't be of much help. And even if I did know how to take care of it, my arm is killing me. I can tell it's not broken, thank God, just badly bruised. Right now I'm not worried about it. It's Christy who I'm really concerned about, because I don't know how long we're going to be stuck up here.

"Christy, can you move your leg?" I ask.

Struggling to hold on to what's left of the chimney, Christy slowly rolls over while keeping a tight grasp on her leg at the same time. "Ow," she grunts. "I think my leg is broken. I can't feel it, except when I move, and then it hurts. Oh my God, it hurts so bad, Angie," she says, whimpering from the pain. "Oh God, help me," she pleads, clutching my good arm with incredible pressure.

"I got you," I say, nervously reaching out to grab her as she cries out for help.

Exhausted from last night's struggle, she rests in my arms, breathing as if all the energy she'd had was taken from her. Then, suddenly, she leans her head back onto my shoulder, seeking comfort. I notice there are tears falling from her eyes, though she doesn't make any sound beyond simply breathing.

Holding her close in my arms, I sit bleakly, wishing all this was just a dream, imagining that at any moment now we might wake up and everything will be okay. But here we are, sitting on a partially submerged roof. So, no matter how much I want to believe otherwise, the dark reality is that everything isn't okay. The hurricane really did hit us, and with my hurt arm and Christy's bad leg, our survival depends on being found and rescued quickly. Unfortunately, we haven't seen any rescue teams, and the helicopter that passed over us this morning didn't see us. I have to say, unless the helicopter comes back, the next few days are going to be tough.

Looking around in stunned disbelief, I notice that our entire house has been swept off its foundation and pushed across the street into our neighbors' front yard. With all the shaking and noise last night, I did not realize that the force of the wind and water had begun shifting our whole house.

The Industrial Canal must have overflowed its banks, and the floodwaters have submerged my entire neighborhood. The only things that are visible are a few rooftops. You can't even see where Gordon Street starts or where it ends. I can only imagine this is what sitting on a deserted island feels like. Aside from rooftops, the only thing in sight for miles is water, with the exception of scattered bits and pieces of debris floating swiftly by with the current.

As we sit here, helplessly, in the scorching sun, time seems to creep by. With nothing but time on our hands and silence surrounding us, I strain to catch any sign of rescue workers.

Much later, I hear what sounds like a helicopter.

"Christy," I ask, waking her. "You hear that?"

"Hear what?" she says.

"Listen."

Listening very hesitantly, Christy softly replies, "To what?"

"You hear that? It's a helicopter," I reply as I scour the sky for signs of movement.

"I don't hear anything." Christy shrugs. "Are you *sure* you hear a helicopter, or are you just hearing things?"

I hold very still, listening, for more than a minute, but I don't hear anything that could be a helicopter. For a moment, my hopes for survival drop, and I have to take a few moments to gather myself together and compose myself. I can't let myself give up, but it is an incredible disappointment to think that I was only hearing things.

Perched as we are on the roof, at least we have a stable place to rest while we keep our eyes and ears alert for signs of people. Time passes slowly. After a while, as I look out into the distance, I notice something resting upon the red brick rooftop of Ida Mae's house, which has been ripped from its foundation and has plowed into another house. I feel a sudden surge of hope, and I squint against the slanted rays of the sun to make sure. Lo and behold, it's Momma. I can't believe my eyes.

Excited, I scream, "Momma, Momma!" I hope she can hear me.

My sudden outburst frightens Christy and causes her to jump.

"Momma? Where?" she asks, hopeful but clearly exhausted.

"Over there, look!" I say, pointing excitedly.

"Momma!" We yell simultaneously, hoping our tired voices will carry across the water. "Momma, Momma!"

After a few minutes of screaming from the top of our lungs, we stop and wait to see if she heard us. But our shouts do not avail us. She's not responding. As we watch, a current dislodges her body from the roof, and she drifts slowly by, facedown in the water. At her closest, she drifts only a few feet away from the house. And next to her, also floating, is the emergency kit Christy and I prepared. We left it behind in the kitchen in our rush to get into the hallway and find a haven from the strong wind.

It's too much. Christy and I break down in tears. I can hear myself saying "No, no," over and over, but I can't make myself stop. I can't believe this. "No, no, no, no," I cry, burying my face in Christy's shoulder. It helps, but only barely.

Too numb to speak, Christy stares at Momma's body as it floats by in the murky water. There's nothing we can do but look on and cry. Just hours ago, I was making every effort to save her, and now it's too late. I can't do anything. I can't remember ever feeling this helpless. What could I have done differently? If I'd been faster, maybe I could have saved her and prevented all this. I can feel a lump in my throat. Breaking down, I bury my head in Christy's arms, crying.

"Why?" I ask. I'm not sure who I'm asking, but I need an answer. "Why?" I can't stop feeling guilty. "Why?" Why did this happen? Why weren't we ready? *What more could I have done?*

Holding me close in her arms, Christy doesn't say a word. She lets me grieve, holds me while I cry.

We sit like that, together, for a long, long time.

The day goes on, of course. The world doesn't stop just because one person's life is over. I'm torn between mourning for Momma and thinking of the future. What would Momma do? Well, she'd figure out a way to keep us alive and safe, that's what she'd do. But it's not that easy. With no clue as to how long we'll be up on the rooftop, it's clear we need supplies. And the emergency kit is there, only a short distance away, floating. Part of me knows I should jump into the water and get the emergency kit so that we can have something to eat and drink. But I'm so tired and worn out, I can't even move to get it. And Christy doesn't know how to swim, so she can't help. Even if she did know how to swim, she couldn't help; her leg is broken. So we're just sitting here, hot, sweaty, dehydrated, and famished from lack of food.

Maybe I'll go after the emergency kit in a little while. When it's a bit cooler. Besides, right now it's floating up against Momma's body, and I'm not about to go out there and pull it away from her. I just can't do it. It's entirely too much to take in right now.

I sit, staring dazedly, my eyes fixated on Momma's body as she floats on by. I hope that the helicopter we've seen flying over stops to rescue us soon, because I can't bear to watch anymore. But at the same time, I can't look away.

As the day continues, the heat intensifies. And the stench of raw sewage begins to pollute the air. Oh, my goodness, the smell! Christy and I wonder aloud how long it'll be before anyone sees us sitting here. How long can we survive without any water or food? I can't help but wonder whether we're going to die here. If the sight of Momma's body alone doesn't make us lose hope, maybe the fear of not being rescued will.

Trying not to overreact, we sit still to preserve energy. Our previous conversation dies, and we sit in silence on top of the roof, neither of us saying a word. There is nothing new to see, and thinking about the future hurts. As my eyes look out over the toxic water, my mind drifts down memory lane.

I reminisce on how Momma would take Mark and me for walks in the neighborhood when we were young. Tears run down my face as the thought of her laughter runs through my mind. And seeing her corpse floating nearby is incredibly painful; a sharp, fresh pain that only grows worse every time I look at it.

I just want to die.

#

Momma would walk Mark and me damn near everywhere she could, because we had no car to really get around in. We couldn't afford one for years and years. I remember how, when we were kids, we'd walk with her to Mr. Green's Grocery. Mark and I were welcomed with open arms, and sometimes Mr. Green acknowledged the two of us with candy. He knew we were Ellyn Johnson's children because we came to the store with her so often to shop.

I can recall those days very vividly. I remember when I was ten and Momma first taught me how to cook. I had to learn so that I could feed Mark each night while Momma worked.

The first thing Momma taught me was how to boil a hot dog, heat up some pork and beans in a pot, and put some frozen French fries in the oven. That was my first self-cooked meal, and I was proud of my hot dogs, pork and beans, and French fries.

While Christy, Tasha and Kimberly were just being kids, having fun and playing outside, I would sit at the table and watch Momma in the kitchen while she cooked. At first, I learned how to make some of the simplest dinners for Momma, Mark and me, and as I grew, I began to learn more complicated recipes.

Some meals required no knowledge of any recipe, as long as the cook had plain common sense. It became easy for me to make cornbread, fried chicken, mashed potatoes, and canned string beans. That was good eating, too. I always made sure I had dinner ready for Momma every night when she came home after a long day of work.

I feel tears sting my eyes at the thought. The last time I cooked like that was two Sundays ago. Who would have thought, just two Sundays ago, that that Sunday would be our last supper together?

Looking out over the Lower 9th Ward, the only thing that stands out is the marquee of Mr. Green's Grocery, still rising proudly above the floodwaters. I guess this really is what it feels like for shipwreck survivors to be stranded on an island, waiting to be saved, not knowing if rescue will come in time or not.

#

"How deep do you think the water is?" Christy asks a few hours later. It is now late afternoon, though I can't tell exactly what hour it is.

"I don't know," I reply. My thoughts tumble over each other, slowly, as I try to answer the question. "A few months ago, Mr. Thompson was telling Momma about his improvement plans for the Lower 9th Ward." He represents the Lower 9th Ward on the City Council, and since I work in City Hall, I see him fairly often. "He'd asked her to get the house appraised so that the city can have an estimate as to how much it will cost to buy her house if his plan was to happen. I read the appraisal, and it gave the dimensions of Momma's house from the ground to the roof as twelve feet, so since part of her roof is submerged I'm guessing the water is at least thirteen feet deep."

"Wow," Christy says, surprised. "That's a *lot* of water." She looks at the small waves lapping against the roof, and I know she's thinking about not being able to swim. With just the tip of Momma's rooftop visible, Christy and I sit uncomfortably on the remaining portion with our legs in the water to help deal with the heat. We revert back to silence, waiting without speaking, even as we try to brush away the red ants that have just recently appeared, trying to crawl up our legs. It's a losing battle. There are so many of them, and we're so tired already.

I break the silence. "How's your leg?" I ask Christy.

"Not good," she replies as she brushes away the red ants. She's clearly in a lot of pain.

Looking around us in dismay, I can't help but feel that our chances are low. "I hope we make it through this," I say, fighting the urge to give in to hysteria. I don't want to die here. "I don't know how long we can sit here without any food or water," I say helplessly.

Holding my hand, Christy consoles me. "We're going to make it. Just hold on," she says.

With tears in my eyes, I shake my head. Not to deny her, but in the hope that something will start to make sense. It doesn't work. "Why, why, why?" I cry out, startling even myself with how loud my voice is. "This just can't be real."

Like a true friend indeed, Christy comforts me with soothing words. "We're not going to give up so easy," she says firmly. "Someone will see us and come rescue us." As she gives me a well-deserved hug, she adds, "You have to stay strong for me, Angie. Momma wouldn't like you giving up on her like this," she says, and now she's crying, too. "We're going to make it, Angie. We *have* to. We can't give up. We can't die like this. We have a bigger purpose in life, and it doesn't involve just sitting here and throwing in the towel," she says fervently.

Despite my near-hysteria, her words strike a chord with me. They resonate in my mind and give me hope for tomorrow. I don't know that tomorrow is going to come, but if nothing else, I won't let myself give up on trying to live. Now that Momma's gone, I feel helpless, like I really have no purpose. As if my life was taken from me the moment she died.

But Momma wouldn't want me to give up, either. Even though I have no idea what to do with myself, Momma wouldn't want me to give in to despair.

What am I going to do without her? Even if the Lower 9th Ward can one day rebuild from this devastation,

[81]

coming home will never be the same. I'm overwhelmed by the thought of never being able to call the Lower 9th Ward home again. The entire neighborhood is gone, lost, destroyed, and there's nothing worth coming back to.

The sight of ravaged houses, waterlogged vehicles, and bloated corpses floating in the water is horrifying beyond words. And to see Momma's corpse floating in the distance is unbelievably saddening. How much more of this can I take? I'm not sure, but even though I've driven off panic for now, I can tell I'm very close to losing it.

#

It doesn't help at all when the emergency crews flying over in helicopters don't hear our cries for help, which worries me even more. When that happens, something small but important shatters inside of me. That moment is when I start to believe that Christy and I are going to die on this roof. I'm not panicking about it anymore, just accepting it. But it's a major change. I used to worry, *What if we are stuck here? What if we die?* Now I don't worry about it. It's going to happen. I won't let Momma down—I'm going to keep myself and Christy alive as long as I can—but I feel like it's just empty gestures at this point. No matter what we do, Christy and I are going to die on this roof.

And the heat is not helping at all. It's hot, which makes our awful conditions even worse. Sweating profusely, I sweep my hand into the water to wash away the ants and I douse my face and upper body with the murky water in an effort to stay cool. Next to me, Christy does the same.

Hot, hungry and dehydrated, I know that survival by any means is imperative. And watching the emergency kit float nearby, the thought of going after it has become more tempting by the minute. If I can get up the strength to get it, at least we'll have something to replenish our bodies. But Lord knows, right now the sun has taken the life out of me, and my arm is still badly bruised. If anything goes wrong, whether I hurt myself on some hidden object or my arm freezes up, I don't know that I'll be able to make it back to Christy. And despite the despair I feel, I don't want to risk leaving her here alone.

"So how long do you really think we'll be here?" I ask.

Christy looks up into the sky before replying. "I wish I knew. We've only seen two helicopters fly over since this morning," she says, frustrated. "If it keeps up like this, who knows?"

"Yeah," I say, looking out over the slowly moving water. I had imagined that we would see dozens of search teams today, especially since we first saw a helicopter early this morning. Now that I think about how huge the city is, I wonder how I could have expected help so quickly. Even if there are tens of thousands of people trying to help us, it will take days or weeks to search every neighborhood, every house.

"I'm not sure how long we can survive out here," I say. Part of me realizes that I've said something similar before, but I would rather listen to Christy's reply than be trapped with my own dark thoughts.

"I'm not sure, either. Besides," Christy moans, "I can't feel my leg, and I'm getting chills." She hunches a little, as if she's protecting herself against a cold draft, but the sun is beating down on us as mercilessly as ever.

"I feel restless," Christy adds. I know what she means. If only we could move around a little. And it's worse for Christy, who has to be extra careful because her leg.

With concern for Christy now foremost on my mind, hunger and dehydration have become the least of my worries. Right now, getting proper medical aid for her leg is my biggest concern, followed next by getting Momma out of this toxic water. I'm not going to leave her here. But God, what can I do to help Christy? This girl is like a sister to me, and right now, when she needs help most, I can't do anything. We've been through a lot of emotional pain growing up, but this takes the cake. She's been my rock and my support when I needed her, through my heartache with my ex-boyfriend Anthony, and the death of Momma's dad and my Big Daddy, William Johnson. And she's been there in tough times to put me in my place and to tell me that I needed to tone my attitude down because not everyone could deal with me.

The hunger and heat are bad, but the worst part of the past day is that all this is finally making me admit that I can't always help the people I love most. I couldn't help Momma, and now, I can't help Christy. At least, I can't help to set her leg or to make the pain vanish. But I *can* help to keep her alive another day or two. It's not nearly enough, but it's something.

#

The heat is intense. Christy and I try to stay focused, so as to not give in to exhaustion, extreme hunger, or thirst. Even though we both seem to be slipping in and out of consciousness, I try to keep talking in an effort to stay alert. *Where,* I ask myself, *are those damn helicopters?*

I look over at Christy. Her eyes are open, but her stare is blank. She is still awake, but just barely. She seems to be slipping away from me, and the thought of losing her too is terrifying. I feel so helpless. I can't do anything to help her or myself. All we can do is keep waiting for help, any kind of help, to arrive.

"Christy?" I call out.

I don't expect her to answer, but I try to watch for any sign that she's still conscious. I hear a faint groan, and I take that for an answer. My mouth is so dry now, I can barely speak myself, but I continue speaking anyway. I try to pretend that it's just like we're on the phone, talking for hours about everyday things, instead of desperately trying to stay awake after our lives have been torn apart. "You remember that fight we had back in elementary school?" I hesitate a second, expecting her to answer. I just keep on talking, trying to make her stay conscious. I don't know if it'll work or not. But I've got to try something.

"You remember?" I continue to ramble. "We were fighting over that boy, Gerald or Jared, or whatever his name was. That was some fight. We were going at it like cats and dogs. It took Ms. Williams and Coach Jackson to pull us apart. And then we had to stay for after-school detention and Ms. Williams made us write, '*I will never fight over a boy again.*' I think we must have written it, what, about a thousand times, didn't we?"

I pause again but Christy doesn't respond. I keep talking, trying my best not to let my fear take over.

"My hand was hurting so bad from all that writing. And when I got home, Momma…" My voice trails off as I think of Momma, with her lifeless body floating face down only a few feet away from us. I can feel my self-control slipping. I can tell I'm about to lose it when suddenly, I hear Christy speak.

"She beat your ass!"

Together, we laugh so hard that I think we have both gone completely hysterical. Here we are, lying on this roof, surrounded by more water than we've ever seen because even on the beach the ocean only makes up half of what you can see. We aren't even sure if we are going to survive. But here we are, laughing our heads off.

"Oh that was funny," I say, after I catch my breath. "I needed that laugh. I haven't laughed like that in a while. I thought you passed out on me."

"No, I heard your crazy butt talking."

"If you did, why didn't you say anything?"

[85]

"I just wanted to see how long you were going to talk," she says, still giggling while clutching her leg. "Oh, that hurts. I need to lie back down."

Rolling my eyes, I reply, "You make me sick. Don't scare me like that."

"Hmm huh," Christy says, lying back on the roof.

With our sudden burst of energy expended, we're back where we started, only now Christy is showing clear signs of fatigue.

Weak and in need of serious medical attention, Christy's responses become slower as her eyes become heavy. She's drifting to the brink of unconsciousness, and I'm not sure she'll come back to me once she's passed over that edge.

"Christy," I say, worried, "wake up. You can't go to sleep, baby. You have to stay up with me. We have to talk about work," I add, reaching out to hold her in my arms. My vision blurs; there are tears in my eyes. "Don't leave me. Come on," I insist, rocking her back and forth.

She doesn't stir. Crying my heart out, now, I lift my head, hoping God will hear my plea. "No," I beg, "not her. You can't take her, too!" Tears are streaming down my cheeks, and I don't care. All that matters is that she's not answering.

And suddenly her eyes roll up. She has fallen limp in my arms.

"No!" I scream, in a long, drawn-out cry. "No, God, no," I wail. "Why, why, why?" I ask, wanting God to hear, wishing He would answer me. "Why me? Christy, baby, don't leave me."

Running my hand gently across her face, God gives me hope, and I exclaim wordlessly as Christy slowly opens her eyes. "What happened?" she whispers, looking up at me through partially open eyes.

Crying tears of laughter, now, I reply by squeezing her tightly with a huge hug. "Oh God, thank You, thank You, thank You, oh Jesus," I whisper, holding her firmly as I wipe away the tears. "You passed out."

"I did?" she asks. "For how long?"

"I don't know."

"What, you thought I died?" she asks, alarmed.

"Yeah, I thought you'd died," I say, sniffling.

"It's not my time," she replies, smiling dimly. "We got work to do."

As day turns to night, we take a minute to talk about the future and the things that lie ahead for us if we are rescued.

"Christy," I say, "this tragic situation has me thinking." I check to see that she's awake and listening, then I go on. "Thinking about how short life really is, and how we can be gone in an instant." I pause, looking around at the wreckage extending out from us in every direction. "Tomorrow is not promised to us," I say, "so who's to say whether we'll make it, or even live to see morning."

With a pained look plainly written on her face, she replies, "Don't say that. We're going to make it, Angie. I promise you we will. Just have faith."

"I don't know," I say miserably. "It feels like all hope is gone. Sitting here on this roof, just watching Momma's body floating there, has me numb. I don't know what to think anymore," I whisper.

Reaching over to comfort me, Christy squeezes my hand and says, "Angie, I'm just as scared as you are. But I know Momma wouldn't want us to give up or stop trying. I *know* it hurts, seeing her in this water." She gestures at the water with her free arm, a helpless, frustrated motion. "But there's nothing we can do about it except hold on. I mean, look," she says, ranting now, "we made it through the storm! Can't you believe? In the midst of the storm, God allowed us to survive *for a reason*, not so we could give up." She pauses, looks out over the flooded water. "I know Momma's looking down on us. And she's not going to let us die on this roof. She knows her children have a brighter future ahead. So she will send someone to get us. She *will*," Christy insists, teary-eyed. "I know she will."

As night falls upon us, darkness sets in. Hungry and dehydrated as we are, we've made it through the day. With still no signs of rescue, Christy and I fight to stay awake just in case we hear something or in case someone comes. If tomorrow's anything like today, I'm not sure how long we can go on. And Christy can't feel her leg, or move it much. I'm not worried about my arm; I'll manage just fine with a bump and a few bruises.

Even though we hope we'll be rescued tomorrow, the thought of food has become my top priority. I tell Christy that if we're not rescued tonight, I'm swimming out first thing in the morning to get the emergency kit, which has now drifted further away from us. I think maybe a house length or two, probably no more. Now I think I should've gotten it earlier today, but I just couldn't move with the heat and the shock of losing Momma. I couldn't bear the thought of swimming in the water with Momma in it, so soon after finding her body. But right now, it's either do, or die.

Chapter 7 - Hard to Say Goodbye

*J*uly 6, 2004

*F*inally, our day of rescue has come. After three days of scorching heat, surrounded by the stench of raw sewage and death, a helicopter arrives. Unfortunately, we learn, it is already close to capacity with survivors from Hurricane Steven, and we're told there's room for only one of us. The other will have to remain behind and wait to be picked up by the next available rescue team.

I tell Christy I'm staying here with Momma, whose body has now become partially bloated and infested with red ants, and I insist that Christy go with the rescue workers. I tell her she needs to go because of her leg, which is in need of serious medical attention.

As if that isn't enough to convince her, the crewmember who is being lowered down from the helicopter to retrieve us screams, "Come on! We have to get you out of here!" When she looks at me, concerned, he adds, "We will send someone back to get your friend."

With the helicopter hovering overhead, a rescue basket is lowered to pick Christy up. "We can't leave both of you out here, we have to take someone. And that someone has to be you," the crewmember explains, screaming over the roar of the helicopter above us. "You have the most severe injury which requires medical attention, and we need to get you to the hospital as soon as possible. You can't stay here another day, or you'll risk losing your leg," he yells.

Christy nods. She will go. Trying not to cry, I give Christy a tearful hug as she's carefully placed into the basket by the crewmember. She tells me she'll see me later, as if we'll see each other tonight or tomorrow at work. Although I don't know where she's going, I can't fathom not seeing her again.

With tears in my eyes, I watch as she's pulled up and in, and then the helicopter takes her away. As the sound fades in the distance, I am abruptly reminded that I'm alone again, surrounded by an eerie silence. The only noise is from the water thumping up against the house, which has been stirred up by the wind from the helicopter. The stillness is unusual and extremely creepy. Silence is normally hard to come by in the Lower 9th Ward. Because of the constant noise of conversation, laughter, music and movement from local residents, the neighborhood never really sleeps, even at night.

In spite of the horrible conditions around me, I made the decision yesterday morning to swim out through the murky water to get the emergency kit so that Christy and I could eat. Christy and I drank all the water except a single bottle and ate most of the tuna and cracker lunch packs last night. So now I'm left to rummage through leftovers, which is still enough to carry me for maybe another day or two. Sitting here waiting to be rescued, I eat sparingly to conserve as much food as I can, hoping the helicopter will come back soon. I'm really hungry, tired and dehydrated, but also fiercely hopeful for the first time in more than a day.

The day passes by with not a soul in sight. As the hours go by, I start to question my actions. Should I have let Christy go? Should I have begged to go with her? Why am I still sitting here? I just don't know. Surely the helicopter should have returned by now.

Frightened by the thought of not being rescued, I start to think again of all the terrible things that might have happened. Maybe the rescue workers forgot about me. Maybe they gave the next rescue team wrong directions, and now I'm going to die here.

Before long, fresh tears are streaming nonstop down my face. "Oh God, why me?" I ask. "I'm too young to die like this. I can't die like this; I can't die up on this roof. Who'll find me?" I ask aloud. "No one will know where to find me but Christy. God, help me."

My words go out over the water. If there's any answer, I can't see it.

#

I've been sitting here for hours now, and not a helicopter in sight. I'm emotionally drained, and weak from the lack of food and water. I feel myself getting weaker as the minutes pass. Exhausted from crying, I lean up against the chimney to rest. My eyes are getting heavier. Turning back and forth, I find a comfortable position, and within minutes I'm asleep.

I dream a dream where I'm visiting Mark and his wife at their home one evening for a nice summer barbeque. Mark has gotten married to my friend Kimberly, and they have two children. Momma and Daddy are there as well. Momma, Kimberly and I are sitting at a patio table underneath the car porch. Daddy is at the barbeque grill, cooking, and we're all laughing and talking and enjoying each other's company.

Suddenly, Mark pulls into the driveway with my husband, Jamal. Jamal walks over to greet all the ladies with a hug, then turns and gives Daddy a firm handshake. And jumping into my lap is my five-year-old daughter. Mark walks over to the patio table with a bag of ice in his hand, then gives all the ladies a hug and kiss also. He walks over and gives Daddy a nice firm manly hug and a handshake.

"You know what you're doing on that grill, old man?" he asks, laughing, as he puts the ice in the cooler.

"Do I know what I'm doing?" Daddy replies. "*You* asked me to cook, remember," he says, laughing while he points the barbeque fork at Mark.

Abruptly, I'm woken up by a man's shout. "Are you okay?" the crewmember yells.

Disoriented, I squint in the direction of the shout only to see a blur of a man kneeling before me. "Jamal! Is that you?" I say, trying to focus on his face. "Where's the baby? Did Mark get the ice?"

"I'm sorry!" the man shouts. "But I'm not Jamal; I'm Lieutenant Bradford with the United States Military! I'm here to rescue you! How long have you been here?"

"I don't know," I whisper, my voice raspy. "What day is it?" I ask, yawning. The man has wasted no time in checking my bruised arm; he is evidently used to giving medical treatment, and in moments, my right arm has been treated and bandaged.

"It's Thursday," he screams as he works.

"Oh God," I say, stretching and readjusting my position on the roof. "I've been here since Sunday."

"Let's get you out of here," he says, and hands me his canteen. "Here, have some water."

I take several gulps of water, then I lift the canteen and pour a little on my head to cool off.

Seeing this, the crewmember laughs. In another minute, he has finished wrapping a bandage around my elbow. "Let me hook you up to this harness so we can get you out of here," he says.

"Thank you," I reply, crying on his shoulder like he's my modern day Prince Charming. "Thank you! I never thought you'd come to rescue me."

With my head buried in his broad, masculine shoulders, he holds me tightly. "I'm here," he says. "It took a while, but I'm here, I got you. I won't let you go until we land," he says sincerely.

Oh, God, it feels so good to have this small piece of security in the form of a harness and a man holding me tightly. It's a confirmation of safety, something I've yearned for in a man since the day Daddy left. Clasping my arms ever-so-tightly around his body, I hold on with eyes closed. It feels like a warm embrace you can just sink into and don't ever want to let go of. Just for an instant, my mind drifts away from the terrible recent events, toward a happy place I haven't visited in over a week.

My wandering mind takes me to serenity with this man. *Could he be the one? Could he be my Mr. Right?* Although I enjoy this short moment of tranquility, it comes to a sudden stop as we make it to the inside of the helicopter.

My first experience of flying in a helicopter comes to an end as we land in Baton Rouge. I'm taken in for treatment at a high school auditorium that's been outfitted as a makeshift medical facility, and there, doctors volunteering their services check my vital signs.

Everything is okay, except for my arm and my overall stress level. The doctor says my arm is healing, just badly bruised, but the stress will last for several months. As for the ant bites, thank God I'm not allergic to them, because I was badly bitten over my entire lower body. The doctor treated me with antibiotics just in case, so I'm going to be okay. After I tell the doctor about seeing Momma get swept away by the storm and then watching her lie before me dead, the doctor says I'll be traumatized for maybe a year or two. His words don't surprise me. Even now that I'm safe again, I almost can't believe what I've been through over the past five days.

Being in a hurricane is incredibly frightening. The experience is something I'll never forget and one I would never wish upon anyone. And sitting here just thinking about it brings tears to my eyes. But the thought of having lost Momma breaks my heart and makes me cry.

I soon find myself being led to an auditorium filled with hundreds of rescued New Orleans residents, and shown where to go to fill out paperwork to be counted as a survivor. Once that is done, I will be able to get assistance from the Red Cross and the Family National Call Center, or FNCC. I have to tell you, it's a sight to see so many people displaced by the storm, many with nothing but the clothes on their back. Too many of them have lost everything they'd ever owned. Just from my own observations, I can tell most of the evacuees are like me, having never owned much of anything to begin with, let alone having had enough money saved to start over. I guess it's safe to say that no one really knows where to start when it comes to helping these folks get back on their feet. To be fair, neither do I. Looking around the auditorium, I see so much grief and confusion on the many faces of the storm's victims, and I know that I must look the same way.

There's an elderly man here who has to be sixty-five years of age at least. He looks good. And he's very aware of his surroundings and what's going on. But he's been sitting here for two days, waiting for his wife to come to the center. The word around the center is that his wife died in the storm. One of the paramedics says that he's in denial and still believes is wife is out there somewhere.

When I ask, the paramedic tells me this is a normal behavior pattern, and many survivors may experience it. And we may try to deny a lot of the facts related to Steven as we try to cope with the devastation and loss. I suppose the elderly gentleman's behavior is just his way of trying to make it through this terrible time.

As I sit waiting for assistance, I notice a very attractive young mother with the prettiest hazel eyes who appears to be in her early twenties. And she's crying her heart out as she rocks her eight-month-old baby back and forth in her arms. Paramedics tell me the baby died due to heat exhaustion and dehydration while waiting for an emergency aid team to come rescue them. And she will not let go of her child, but breaks down in tears as a doctor comes over to take the baby away. My heart goes out to her and to everyone here who has lost a loved one.

I can't help but cry. This is entirely too much for anyone to bear. If only they knew my story about Hurricane Steven, and I knew theirs, we could help each other more easily. I'm sure everyone here has an incredible story to tell. Right now, though, no one is here to listen to my story and to worry about me. They all have a situation of their own to worry about.

It feels good just sitting here in this air-conditioned auditorium. The rooftop of Momma's house was unbearably hot. It felt like the sun was literally aiming its heat at me to make me suffer, and I have one hell of a sunburn. If that's what hell feels like, then I'm definitely not interested in going.

I grow more concerned as I wait. I can't help but think about where Christy and Mark could be. So, as my concern grows, I walk over to a Baton Rouge policeman who's standing near the auditorium entrance, and say, "My best friend and my brother are missing. Would you know how I can find them?"

"Check the list of names over on the wall," the officer replies, directing me to a bulletin board near the restroom. "The Family National Call Center has posted this list of all the people who have been rescued and brought to this location," he says confidently. "If they're not at this location, let's hope to God they're at another one."

Slowly, I make my way over to the list, which is surrounded by a crowd of survivors looking for loved ones. I notice a pretty little white girl about seven years old standing there in front of the list crying, with her hands covering her face. It appears she's alone and can't find her parents, because she steps back and kneels against the wall, then buries her head between her legs as she continues to cry.

Taking heed of her pain, tears rush down my face as I make that walk to the list to find out if Christy and Mark are here. But it's to no avail; their names are missing. So I walk away, forcing myself to walk with my head high. With tears in my eyes, I hold on tight to my faith, knowing Christy is safe and sound somewhere. And Mark will turn up somewhere alive. He has to. Or am I only in denial, too? I don't know what to think.

Carefully, I walk over to console the little girl, who's now sobbing uncontrollably. "Hi," I say, kneeling beside her. "What's your name?"

Raising her head slowly, her eyes wet with tears, she says, "Megan."

"Hi Megan, my name is Angela," I say. "Is this where pretty little girls come to cry?" I ask. She looks at me with her adorable big blue eyes. "If so," I add, "can I join you?"

"Yes," she says sweetly. Sitting on the floor, I place my right arm around her. She rests her head on my shoulder, and together we sit, crying and waiting for our loved ones to appear. I feel myself falling into a daze as I think about Momma, Christy and Mark, and everything around me fades away into silence.

#

I'm woken some time later, when the Red Cross and Army Reserve pass out food so everyone can eat. But I'm too stressed to eat anything.

Looking at the meal, I wonder if I'm even hungry. I know I need to eat something, but my stomach feels like it won't keep anything down. When I attempt to take several bites, I have to struggle to even swallow. I guess these last few days of not eating much of anything but tuna, crackers, and water have altered my appetite.

Trying not to waste the chicken salad sandwich, potato chips, and pickle, I keep the orange soda, but pass the rest on to Megan, who gladly accepts. With no idea of when we can all return home, we wait in the auditorium hoping for any kind of news. So far we haven't heard anything and the efforts to locate the missing aren't being announced. While the Red Cross does all it can to assist with the seemingly impossible task of finding loved ones in spite of the chaos, we are told that a Hurricane Steven survivor has taken matters into their own hands and started a missing persons list. Upon the bulletin board is now a handwritten list of names of missing loved ones, which I add Megan's parents' names to, as well Mark and Christy.

Later, when I'm watching the television for the first time in days, I'm finally able to see the devastation Hurricane Steven left behind in New Orleans. I've never seen my beloved New Orleans in so much turmoil. Everything is flooded or damaged or destroyed. The levee systems breached and collapsed, causing massive flooding throughout the city. Buildings that previously had stood the test of time, such as the beautiful convention center and aquarium, are now torn beyond recognition due to the heavy wind, and the River Walk on the great Mississippi River is unrecognizable. It's amazing and terrible to see. The news of the incredible devastation is shocking. There's nothing but water everywhere. The entire city is underwater.

With the news heavy on our minds, Megan and I walk over to a nearby bench in the auditorium to sit down. In shock and disbelief, I place my hands over my face to hide my tears. I can't believe what I've just gone through. And from what I've seen so far in the news, New Orleans looks bad. I can't believe that just this past weekend, the city I love was so vibrant with music and people. Now it's not alive with anything anymore. The heartbeat of the city has died, and its last breath was taken the day Hurricane Steven hit. And aerial footage of the Lower 9th Ward doesn't appear to be any better. Megan consoles me and places her arm around me. "You can't cry here. Pretty little girls cry over there," she says, pointing toward the hallway where the bulletin board hangs.

Sniffling, I wipe away my tears, smiling as I hug her. "You're right. Pretty little girls cry over there."

"Are you crying because you miss your mommy and daddy too?" she asks innocently. I haven't told her about Momma.

"Yeah," I say, teary-eyed. "I'm crying because I miss my mommy and daddy too." I know I won't see Momma again anytime soon, and Lord knows if I'll see Daddy either. I haven't seen him since I visited his house Uptown several weeks ago.

"Me too," Megan says. "I miss my daddy more," she says sadly. "He's in the Army, far away from here. He's been gone for a long time. My mommy told me he was coming home Sunday, but I guess the hurricane came home before he did, and I'm waiting for my mommy to come and get me so we can go."

"So where did your mommy go, baby?" I ask, concerned.

"She left," Megan says.

"She left to go where?"

"She left to go pick my Grammy up, so we can leave to go meet Daddy at the Army base. She said it would be a lot safer there when the hurricane came," she replies, crying.

Poor baby, I think. My heart just took another dive. I hope to God this woman didn't mean to leave this child. I just hope she was going to pick up Megan's Grammy and was going to come back like she said. And if she was, I hope to God she made it somewhere safe before Steven hit. Or if she died, I hope she died trying to get back to this child. I just don't understand how she could leave her child alone like this.

"So how did you get here?" I ask.

"The policeman came and got me. He said the hurricane was coming and he had to get me out of my house before it came. I told him I was waiting on my mommy to come back and get me so we can go meet my daddy at the Army base. He asked where mommy was and I told him she went to get Grammy and she'll be back. He said he'll be back to check on me and if mommy isn't back, he'll have to get me to a safe place. That's how I got here," she says, with her head hung low.

"So, your mommy never came back to get you." I sigh.

"No," she says, weeping. "She left me."

Holding her in my arms, I hug her close to my heart. "No, baby. No, she didn't leave you. How could anyone leave such a pretty little girl like you?" I say, while wiping the tears from her eyes. "She's coming back. She just went to get your Grammy, okay, so the three of you can go meet your daddy at the Army base. So wipe your eyes for me and be a big girl. You got to be pretty for him when you go meet him, okay?"

"Okay," she replies, sobbing.

"Okay, that's a big girl," I say, helping her clean up.

"You have to look pretty, too, so you can see *your* mommy and daddy," she says, reaching out to wipe the tears from my eyes.

Crying tears of laughter, I reply, "Yeah, I have to look pretty, too."

While doing my best to comfort Megan, I'm overtaken by the thought of never seeing Momma again. Within minutes I'm having flashbacks of Saturday night and I'm gazing off in the distance, eyes turned to the auditorium but looking elsewhere. As vividly as in a Hollywood blockbuster movie, I'm tuned in to when the storm hit, and every moment is replayed in my mind. I shake in fear as Saturday night plays over and over again, and I'm overcome by emotion. Crying my heart out, I bury my face in my shaky hands to cover my swollen eyes and to hide my tears. I nervously tap my feet on the auditorium floor, trying my best to fight the constant tears.

And in her sweet compassionate way, Megan touches my heart. She gives me a warm hug, which breaks though my daze and helps me relax. "You have to stay pretty for your mommy and daddy," she says softly, as she again wipes away the tears.

I just melt in her arms. "You're right, baby," I say, pulling myself together. "I have to stay pretty for my mommy and daddy."

Taking a deep breath, I take Megan to the little girls' room. While we're walking, she holds my hand for comfort. As weird as this feels, it's like I'm walking with my own child. In a situation like this, I can't imagine being a parent, not knowing where my child could be. I can't think of why her mother would really leave her alone. Why didn't she take Megan with her? When I become a mom, I swear to God I'm going to be the best parent ever. I'm sure that's what they all say, but really, how could anyone be a bad parent to a precious child like Megan? And I know me; Momma raised me well, and having watched her raise Mark and me, I do believe I'll do okay. Thinking about it has me wanting a family of my own one day.

Coming out of the restroom, I take a peek at the bulletin board to see if anything has changed. Nothing has, really, but the list of missing people has gotten longer and the list of survivors has been updated since I last checked for Mark and Christy.

As we're walking back to our seats, Megan and I are met by a group of Army personnel coming into the auditorium with cots, blankets, water, and food. We stand against the wall to get out of their way so they can do their jobs.

During the mayhem of the next few hours, new survivors are brought in while the Family National Call Center and the Red Cross volunteers continue to assist other survivors as quickly as possible. Inside the auditorium among the survivors, it's like total chaos, and no one knows what's happening or where to go from here.

News is now circulating that three to five levees broke, which is why the city is underwater. The worst area for casualties is Interstate 10, where hundreds of cars are sitting underwater and some of the people were trapped inside by the floodwaters.

Hundreds or thousands of bodies are said to be floating in the city. Bodies are everywhere. Rumor has it that when the levees broke, water rushed in like a raging river, crashing into and toppling buildings like dominos and sweeping up everything in its path. The news is coming in from every news reporter across the nation, and very quickly, the rumors about when the levees broke are confirmed.

Information is passed on to law enforcement from the fire marshals about what to do with the overflow of survivors coming in the auditorium. Word is getting around that we may have to be moved due to causing a fire hazard. The place is packed to capacity, and more hurricane survivors come in with each new hour. I've never seen so many distraught people. I hope I never will again. New groups of aid workers and military personnel come in on a regular basis, bringing more supplies or relieving the people who have been here all day. One small group of Army men comes in, and I watch as they start passing out more blankets to survivors who have just arrived.

Then, in a flash, Megan breaks free from my hand and darts into the middle of the soldiers handing out supplies. I look around frantically, but I can't see where she went.

That's when I hear her scream.

"Daddy!" she cries, jumping into her daddy's muscular arms. Shocked by Megan's sudden appearance, the handsome military man dressed in Army fatigues drops the water bottles he was holding in his hands and lifts her up high.

"Oh my God," he says, hugging her tightly. Even from here I can see that he, too, has tears in his eyes. "Oh my God, Megan. Look at you. I can't believe it. You're here. Oh baby, Daddy's so glad to see you." He plants a huge kiss upon her cheek and she buries her head into his shoulder, crying. Around him, some of his buddies cheer and start clapping. They must have seen firsthand how anguished her daddy was, working to help survivors day after day without any sign of his beloved daughter.

Leaning up against the wall for support, I watch as Megan is reunited with her daddy. In the midst of the crowd gathered in the lobby of the auditorium, I cry, wishing my own daddy would come hug me again like he used to when I was four. Touched by the heartwarming scene in front of me, I kneel down next to the wall where pretty little girls cry. Just that quickly, the sweetest little girl has touched my life and vanished, never to be seen again. So here I sit, shaking, with my hands covering my face, as I bury my head between my legs and cry.

Chapter 8 - Moment of Truth

*J*uly 10, 2004

A week has passed since Hurricane Steven hit New Orleans. City, state, and government officials frequently broadcast updates about the conditions of the city, which aren't getting better. News has been announced of the latest casualties recovered. The death toll is worse than I had first thought; it has risen upwards to eight hundred and twenty five, with damages estimated to be in the billions of dollars. These are rough estimates given by Mayor Anthony Jones and Governor Ashley Brown, who're saying that it's going to take maybe a year or two to get New Orleans back on its feet again.

At the present time, the Army Corps of Engineers is saying that the water is draining slowly due to debris in the drainage system. And many of the pumps created to drain the water out of the city have malfunctioned due to excessive water intake. The cleanup and recovery process is scheduled to get underway as soon as the floodwaters recede, which appears to be never. Looking at news footage of the flooding, the water doesn't appear to be draining out of the city at all. A news reporter from Houston traveled the city by boat on Tuesday and measured the waterline against the Merlin building in the French Quarters. From her calculations, the reporter judged the waterline to have been at least sixteen feet deep.

City and state officials strongly believe that the city can rebound and be up and running in time for professional football's big event at the Mega Dome next year. I don't know that their objective is solely to make that happen, but listening to them, I haven't heard a word about what they're going to do about the residents who call New Orleans home.

As for me, right now I don't know if I'm coming or going. I haven't been sleeping well; I toss and turn in bed. And I don't have an appetite, so eating is a struggle. Day in and day out, I'm plagued with recurring thoughts of that night. That Saturday night took everything in my life that I held dear, and I'm wondering how I will go on living without Momma, Mark or Christy.

I haven't heard from Christy or Mark at all, and it's killing me inside. A doctor volunteering at the shelter tells me that my blood pressure is high. I know it; I'm stressed beyond belief. I'm a nervous wreck. I'm not a smoker, but sometimes I feel the urge to smoke a cigarette just to calm myself. *Why not?* I ask myself. It seems to be the thing of choice for other survivors to help them cope with the heartache and pain that Steven has caused.

Today, the President flies over to tour the city from his helicopter. This is his first visit since the storm occurred a week ago. According to the news, he was told about Hurricane Steven's destruction the day after Steven hit the Gulf Coast, destroying large areas of Louisiana, Mississippi, and Alabama.

But President Riley decided to wait a few days before arriving to view the damage. He was busy attending a Peace Summit in South Africa. I suppose he was busy planning his big speech, thinking of what he'd say to

America about any plans the government has for rebuilding New Orleans in a year.

#

While I wait to hear about Christy or Mark, I have a lot of time on my hands to think about the disaster. The thought of America rushing to the aid of other countries and trying to clean up the mess in their backyards makes me wonder. Why are we always late to clean up the mess in our own backyard? This is just my own opinion, but listening to the other survivors in this shelter, many people feel like President Riley's to blame for the delay in medical, water and food assistance, which I heard came two days after the hurricane. And others say that the city of New Orleans and the Louisiana state government are at fault as well, for sending a last-minute evacuation notice the day of the storm, when they could've warned us four days early and saved so many lives.

But I can understand why they didn't, because Steven's path was frequently changing, and the weatherman wasn't able to determine an exact location for where Steven would hit, which was one of the major reasons for the late warning. I understand the weathermen aren't always one hundred percent accurate with their forecasts, but I do agree with those who say they could've done a better job with the tracking of Steven. At least we'd have known what to expect as more information came in.

And I know something many of my fellow survivors don't. None of them was ever aware of the evacuation drill Mayor Jones emailed the City Council about three months ago, which could've been a lifesaver for the city.

The drill outlined detailed evacuation routes in case a hurricane as powerful as Camille should hit New Orleans again. It showed how and where to evacuate, what alternative routes to take out of the city, how to advise everyone without causing pure pandemonium, and how to get everyone to cooperate. And none of this happened.

I suppose Mr. Thompson, the city council member representing the Lower 9th Ward, never received the email. I want to believe that he never got it, because the evacuation drill was never announced to the city. The mayor emailed Mr. Thompson and the city staff three months ago informing everyone of the evacuation drill, which was scheduled in May. And at the time, the plan was a Priority One notice—high on the list. Where the ball was dropped, I don't know, but someone dropped the ball. And how Mr. Thompson didn't receive that email is a mystery to me, because working as I do as an administrative assistant for the New Orleans City Hall, even I received the email about the Hurricane Evacuation Plan.

Many of the New Orleans residents I've talked to, including myself, feel like no one cared enough to bother evacuating the Lower 9th Ward. Maybe if some of the city council had cared more, the death toll wouldn't be eight hundred and rising. My God, I hope and pray that Mark isn't a part of that number. That would break my already-torn heart even more.

But then I wonder, too, can we really blame the city government for the delay in rescuing us, when we should be at fault as well for not evacuating? Instead of trying to weather the storm and hope for the best like always, we should've attempted to leave. Somehow. We should have tried to find a way. That thought leads to others. We knew a hurricane was threatening the Gulf Coast, of course. But what were the chances of us leaving when a majority of the people in the city had no reliable transportation to help them get anywhere? If only we'd known that the city had a plan in place to use its public transportation to evacuate, a lot of us wouldn't even be in this situation—waiting to be rescued or to be placed in makeshift refugee camps, or mourning loved ones. Now ninety-five percent of New Orleans residents are without homes or are missing loved ones because of poor decisions made on their behalf by the city and state governments.

When I think about it looking at all sides, I believe we let our own selves down. We're all at fault. And we have no one to blame but ourselves.

Chapter 9 - A New Beginning

*J*uly 16, 2004

*A*rriving in Atlanta shows me a whole new world. The journey here has been an experience in itself, for a lot of us are flying in an airplane for the first time, and few of us have visited the city before. Often known as the Black Mecca of the South, Atlanta is home to several Historically Black Colleges and many African American civil rights leaders. One renowned leader still has a house here that's frequently visited by tourists.

The pilot announces our arrival over the cabin's loudspeakers. The Red Cross volunteers and Atlanta city officials wait in the airport to welcome our arrival. Charter transportation and police officers wait to escort us to a housing center in the inner city, and I admit I'm nervous to have arrived without any family.

As we enter onto the interstate, we pass a sign that reads, "Welcome to the city of Atlanta! – Barbara Haywood, Mayor." I'm on one of five charter buses that are driving in unison. The city, even seen from the inside of the bus, is beautiful. Arriving as we did around one o'clock in the afternoon, Eastern Time, I'm able to take advantage of the bright sunlight to view the city as we drive by. I just wish Momma, Christy and Mark were here to share this moment with me.

Even though two weeks have passed, I feel a few tears run down my face while I'm looking out of the huge bus window. The glare from the sun makes my reflection clear on the glass as I stare outside, daydreaming about New Orleans. Here I am, heading for a new life in a city sprawling with economic empowerment, but I don't have any idea about what's coming next. And I must admit, I'm frightened to be here alone. How can I even begin to fit into a city so big, one that's already overpopulated, with over two hundred thousand people living in it? I guess I'll find that out in the next couple of hours, or maybe the next few days. I hope I'm able to get assistance immediately so I can start to make something new of my life.

My daydreaming is cut short by the sight of the city skyline. I must say that New Orleans has never looked this big. The buildings here are at least sixty to seventy stories high. You'll never see a building that is this tall in New Orleans; our soil isn't solid enough to build a foundation on it that could withstand that kind of height. The soil there is so saturated with water; anything this tall would sink or fall over.

Looking out the window at the city I'm to live in, I'm somewhat in awe of the view. It's truly breathtaking. I've heard a lot about Atlanta, but never did I imagine the city to be this beautiful. And from the looks on the faces of the parents and children that were rescued from New Orleans, I can tell they agree. I keep hearing the amazed children talk about how big the buildings are. Thanks to the bus driver, we're able to get a first-hand tour of the city, as she announces area landmarks whenever we pass one by.

We pass Emmanuel Hospital while driving on Interstate 75. The hospital serves the two surrounding counties of Fulton and DeKalb. I can only imagine what it's like to go there for an emergency. The hospital appears to be so huge that it may take all day just to be seen. But I guess that's the way it is when your hospital has to provide services to the general public of two metro counties.

When we enter the housing center, which sits just off the interstate, Red Cross officials greet us and direct everyone to a check-in area. This facility is much bigger than the Baton Rouge center, which was located in a high school gym and held around one hundred people, or maybe a few more than that, including some children. It was a little crowded during the four days I stayed there, to say the least. Especially considering that more and more evacuees were being sheltered there with each day that passed.

With the gym becoming seriously overcrowded, local Red Cross and Baton Rouge government officials finally came to the conclusion that they should transport everyone to Atlanta, where the survivors could live in a more permanent shelter. I guess they thought it would be in our best interest to try something new. Some of us fought not to come, wanting to stay there and wait for news of loved ones. But here we are.

As I approach the registration desk, I'm greeted by a Red Cross volunteer who happens to be a sweet and very helpful white woman. She appears to be in her mid-to-late fifties, and she reminds me of Momma in so many ways that her behavior actually startles me. From the way she smiles and wears her glasses, even down to the way she speaks with a Creole accent, everything she does reminds me of home.

"Hello and welcome to Atlanta," she says graciously. "My name is Rebecca Stanley," she adds, extending her hand. "And you are?"

Smiling for the first time in a long time, I reply, "Angela Johnson."

"Well, nice to meet you, Angela Johnson," Ms. Stanley says. Ms. Stanley and I talk for a little while about New Orleans. She wants to know more about me. Apparently when she first saw me, she thought I was one of the prettiest things she's ever seen. And she said I reminded her of her niece, who has a warm, vibrant, and inviting spirit. She tells me that she can sense that in me as well.

Several times during our conversation, I catch myself crying a bit, just thinking about my childhood growing up in New Orleans. As we speak about my past, I realize that my memories are powerful but also touched by sadness. To think it's all gone is heart-wrenching. And the number of homes and families that have been torn apart is tragic.

Noticing the tears running down my face, Ms. Stanley hands me a piece of tissue to wipe away the tears.

"Thank you," I say.

Then she looks at me like Momma would and clutches my right hand.

"God bless you," she says compassionately. "Listen—I know you've been through so much in the past couple of weeks. I just want to tell you that my heart goes out to you and to everyone affected by the tragedy of Hurricane Steven. I know there isn't much I can do to make things better, but if you need anything, I'm here, honey. Anything to help you through this moment. My door's always open," Ms. Stanley says, passing me her business card, which has her name and number printed on it.

"Thank you," I say sincerely. I leave the registration desk and head toward an entire new start on life. Having given Ms. Stanley my name, social security number, and last known address so she can start processing my request for emergency aid, I am led by Red Cross volunteers into a coliseum the size of a football field. There, I'm told, I should be able to find every sort of assistance I might need, from housing, employment, education, and financial assistance, to donations of clothes, food, and medical services. Everything is already in place to help us.

The Red Cross is seeing to it that whatever anyone might need is in one building. It's a one-stop shop. At first I don't know where to start, and I'm pulled in every direction, trying to fill out forms for all the different types of assistance I need.

Ms. Stanley is a big help to me. By going to my bank's website, Ms. Stanley obtains my bank statements for me and contacts the bank's corporate branch in Chicago. The branch manager asks me for my name, account information, date of birth and social security number for security purposes before I am allowed to access my checking and savings accounts or withdraw money.

Once all the information is verified, I am given access to the money in my account. It isn't much; only a few hundred dollars. But it's just enough to help buy a few vital items, like phone cards so I can contact distant relatives from Arkansas to let them know I'm okay, health care products such as deodorant, soap, and toothpaste, and feminine hygiene products. Hopefully the few hundred dollars I have will carry me though the long process of recovering from Hurricane Steven. If not, I'll just have to beg and borrow, which my pride finds so hard to do. Hopefully, if things go badly, my relatives in Arkansas will be able to let me stay out there for a while. I don't know, though. We'll just have to wait and see.

Ms. Stanley also helps me with getting clothes, since my wardrobe has become limited to four shirts, three pairs of pants, and a single pack of panties and socks which I received from the donation station when I was in Baton Rouge.

As far as housing arrangements go, I'm placed on a list for Section 8 housing, which I have to patiently wait for. Who knows how long that could take? Until then, I'll take life one day at a time, focusing on food, medical care, and finding a job. From the look of things, it's going to be a long stay here at the housing center, for me and for many others. But for now, I'm just happy to be in the company of my fellow New Orleans residents, and to have met Ms. Stanley, my newfound friend from Atlanta. It really is true what they say about Atlanta's residents: they definitely greet you with warm southern hospitality.

Chapter 10 - The Latest Update

August 5, 2004

A month has gone by since Hurricane Steven struck the Gulf Coast. I've been on an emotional roller coaster ride lately. As I go through the motions of starting a new life, my mood shifts and I'll often find myself sitting alone in the housing center, depressed and uncertain. With no family members or friends to speak to, I'll find myself crying from grief or simple loneliness.

There's no pattern to it. One day I'm just as cheerful as ever, and the next day I'm having flashbacks of the Fourth of July. Once the flashbacks begin, all these sad thoughts rush at me at once. Suddenly, I'll be saddened by the thought of that day, because so many lives were lost, including Momma's. Then I'll hurt to think that her body may still be floating in the water, or I'll feel terrible because she may never receive a proper burial.

My emotions are often triggered by news updates. Every time I watch the news, the biggest story is always about Hurricane Steven, so I'm constantly reminded of that horrific day. You can't help but to listen to the news, because it seems like every minute there's another update informing every one of the latest conditions in New Orleans. It seems like the media outlets can't stop talking about how the pumps failed, the levees broke, and how the death toll has risen. And they constantly remind me that it may take weeks before all the water flooding the city can completely drain out.

I wasn't able to get up from my sleeping cot due to depression on several occasions this past month. I'd just lie there, watching the news and wondering about my future. Ms. Stanley would worry about me not getting up and she'd come to my sleeping cot to talk and try to cheer me up. She told me all the time that I couldn't just lie there and watch television all day. She said it's not healthy, and that so much television will hinder my ability to think clearly and make it hard for me to pay attention to life. I don't know about that—I keep watching the news anyway. But I don't think she'd tell me anything that wasn't for my own good.

Ms. Stanley is becoming a very special person in my life. She keeps me focused on moving forward. Whether I stay here in Atlanta or move to New Mexico or Arkansas, it doesn't matter to her; she'll be real supportive of any decisions I make. But regardless of what I say, I just want to be back home in New Orleans. There's no other place like my hometown. From the look of things televised on the news, though, my chances for returning soon aren't looking good.

The news media has been depicting New Orleans as a hazardous waste site because of all the ruined homes and raw sewage spills. No one but city or government officials, local authorities, contractors, and federal aid workers are allowed inside the city. Some of those are visiting in order to assess the damage in preparation for when the water recedes, then they will start efforts to clean up debris and recover bodies from the devastation Hurricane Steven left behind.

I can tell that I'm handling my losses better as time goes on, though reminders are everywhere. Pictures of Steven's destruction, posted several times a week in the local newspaper, are enough to make any person feel compassion for the people of New Orleans during this tragic time, and it's so much worse for those survivors like myself who saw the damage firsthand. Oftentimes now, I'll turn the television off when the news comes on because I can't bear seeing any more of the live media updates. It's heartbreaking to see one's home like that, knowing that it's not possible to return.

Since my arrival in Atlanta, the news has been the only thing I've watched on television. On the one hand, I want to stay current and informed. I want to know what's going on and to see how the daily progress is going, but I don't want to become so overwhelmed by the destruction the media outlets show. I now attempt to watch as little as possible while still staying updated, but it's a never-ending story.

The latest news update says President Riley is re-visiting the flooded areas and has plans to tour the city once more by boat. The last time the President visited was a week after the storm, when he viewed the flooding of New Orleans from Marine One, his personal helicopter. I'm waiting to see what he has to say this time, after he has taken a closer look at the city.

A lot of Hurricane Steven evacuees, including me, would like to know what's going on in New Orleans now that preparations are underway for cleanup and recovery. What we're hearing from Governor Ashley Brown and Mayor Anthony Jones is that there aren't enough city workers to start cleaning the city and its surrounding parishes. A massive cleaning, from what we're told, will not start until the water fully recedes. However, the city has begun to slowly filter some of the water to help prepare for the cleanup process and to recover some of the decomposed corpses lying around the city.

It sounds as though it could be years before everyone who once lived there can return to New Orleans. And what can we expect when we do return home, if and when we are able to? Sitting on the rooftop of Momma's house during the four days after Steven hit, I didn't believe anyone could return to the Lower 9th Ward. The footage shows that my neighborhood is still flooded, which doesn't raise my hopes any. And I don't believe anyone could just return to the city, either. Maybe it will be possible after the cleanup efforts get underway, but right now, I don't see it.

Yesterday, I searched on the Internet for aerial footage of New Orleans. Looking at the satellite imagery was amazing. It was scary to see the Gulf of Mexico and New Orleans conjoined; it looked like the entire city was one huge lake running into the Gulf Coast. With so much water having overtaken the city, I have to wonder how anyone expects the city to return to normalcy.

New Orleans Mayor Anthony Jones and Louisiana Governor Ashley Brown have appeared live on CGN News several times to give brief statements about the progress in New Orleans. It's always the same story: nothing can be done until all of the water has receded. The Mayor, Governor, and President are all talking about the same thing. And money is the biggest issue. Each government official seems to be more concerned about who's footing the bill for disaster relief than about the people who were displaced. The Mayor and Governor are asking for billions of dollars in federal aid. The President is asking the state and city to pay half, an amount which neither the state nor the city can afford. So it's just a mess. It doesn't matter to me who pays, though, as long as progress is made. Each bureaucracy could split the tab and pay a portion for all I care, as long as work gets done. Besides, I'm more concerned with problems like Mark's safety and recovering Momma's body so that I can give her a proper burial. As for Christy, I know she's safe. I just don't know where.

Yesterday, I sent the Lower 9th Ward's city councilman, Mr. Thompson, an email. I told him I was concerned about the city pulling together. I also told him that I was doing fine in Atlanta, and that I'm ready to come home to get Momma. He emailed a reply telling me that things are going slowly. The city can't start to recover any bodies until the water fully recedes. He said as soon as the city gives permission to go into the Lower 9th Ward to start the cleanup and recovery process, he'll make sure Momma's body is one of the first to be recovered. But because the water is filthy and contaminated with bacteria, sludge, and raw sewage, precautionary measures must be taken when searching for bodies in those hazardous conditions.

Even when I don't think about the New Orleans recovery projects, I have plenty to worry about. Oftentimes I just sit on my cot, wondering how hard it will be to get back on my feet after all of this. I wish I knew how long it will take. The Red Cross has been a tremendous help. Thanks to their generosity, at least I can say I have gotten some help, even if it's just a little in comparison to what I once had. Regardless, any help is appreciated. Believe me, I feel fortunate; I could still be in New Orleans waiting to be rescued. Or I could have been one of the less fortunate, and died while waiting. Thank God I was spared that, at least.

But the Red Cross can't perform their civic duty without the charitable contributions of hardworking people like Jamal Davenport, who has been willing to give monetarily to help the cause.

A recent news update has it that Jamal, who still plays baseball for the Miami Blue Fins, has pledged to donate one million dollars of his earnings from one game to the Hurricane Steven Relief Fund. He's also helping to raise money by running a charitable auction in each city the team plays in over the next few months. It brings a smile to my face to know there's someone who's so supportive of this cause. I always knew Jamal had a good heart. And to think that Christy and I had just seen him the day before Steven made landfall! I'm glad he was able to get out of town in time before Steven hit.

Chapter 11 - One Autumn Day

*S*eptember 6, 2004

*F*inally, after spending the past two months seeking employment, I get a job interview with one of America's most prestigious hotel chains. Now I'm able to adventure out into Atlanta for the first time, thanks to Ms. Stanley, who gave me directions to the hotel where I will be interviewed today. Like a tourist, I'm overwhelmed at first by the sights of the city, and also by its lovely weather. It's nice, not too hot or too cold, but just right to walk around in. Trust me—it's not anything like New Orleans on a brisk fall day, but it'll do. I've heard before that Atlanta's weather can be scorching hot in the summer and frigid cold in the winter, but today the weather feels great.

Despite Ms. Stanley's directions, I've never been to the hotel and I'm without a clue as to what sort of building to look for. Apparently Atlanta's hotels, like so many other buildings here, are tall and full of glass windows. So the majority of my time is spent walking up and down Atlanta's famous Peachtree Street, looking lost. But even so, just to be in such a historical city, exploring my new surroundings, is refreshing. However, it's apparent I don't know where I'm going. Wandering effortlessly, I approach a young lady name Gloria McDonald, an Atlanta native who sees my confusion for help. "Excuse me, but I'm looking for the Bobby Allison building, can you show me where it's located, please? I've been walking up and down this street for a while, and I can't seem to find it." Gloria kindly smiles, "Sure, if you walk back down this way just a bit and past this building, it's the tall building on the left. You might've walked past it several times without knowing it." She kindly points me in the direction, where I'm able to look up and see that the building is literally right in from of me. Looking up in the direction to which she pointed, I couldn't help but to laugh and shake my head in disgrace.

I'm embarrassed to say it, but I've walked past the hotel building twice already. Entering the spacious lobby of the Allison Building, I'm amazed by how inviting and impressive everything is. The décor is breathtaking. Marble has been laid in an asymmetrical pattern throughout the floor of the lobby. And in the center, a lovely marble water fountain spews water from two beautiful male and female statues. The lighting placement is radiant. High above, the forty-foot ceiling features a massive gold-plated chandelier that is lit up like the sun. It has to be at least eight feet wide.

Walking to the directory board, I locate the Trinity corporate office on the fortieth floor. Who could've imagined so many law firms: realtors, advertising companies, sports and management agencies, and prominent insurance and entertainment companies could be in one building?

When I ask, security tells me that the builder, Bobby Allison, owns a majority of Atlanta's skyline and much of the residential property in the city. By looking at the directory, I learn that his company, Bob Allison Properties, is on floors forty-five through fifty. Rumor has it his company is donating an entire building in order to house Hurricane Steven evacuees. If that were true, I wouldn't mind being one of the lucky few selected to live in one of the Bob Allison Properties homes, which I hear are really nice.

Taking the elevator to the fortieth floor is a scary feeling. I've never been so high in a building before. Butterflies race through my stomach as I rise high above the city skyline. The feeling gives me chills and makes me feel nauseated, but as soon as the elevator stops, I step out onto the solid floor and feel much better.

Entering the receptionist's lounge, I'm greeted by a very handsome and attractive young man named Carl who appears to be in his mid-twenties. He smiles brightly and says, "Hello, and welcome to Trinity Corp. How can I help you?" I can tell he loves his job.

"Hello," I say with a smile. "I'm here to see Mr. Vincent Bedford. I have an interview scheduled with him at two o'clock."

"Okay, can you have a seat please? Mr. Bedford will be with you shortly," Carl tells me kindly.

Taking a seat in a nearby leather armchair, I wait for Mr. Bedford's arrival. Out the corner of my eye, I can't help but notice Carl watching me as I wait. Trying not to make eye contact with him, I marvel at the beautiful layout of the office. Paneled in mahogany wood with a black and gold trim that matches the black marble floor, the lounge is a spectacular example of craftsmanship. The interior design resembles some of Trinity's finest hotels.

Suddenly a tall, dark and handsome man with a confident walk appears. Carl makes him aware that I'm here to see him for the two o'clock interview.

Mr. Bedford graciously walks over to greet me. "Ms. Johnson," he says with a smile, "how are you doing?"

"Fine," I say, as I extend my hand to greet him.

"Did you have any trouble finding us?" he asks.

"A little, but someone was nice enough to help me get here," I reply.

"Well, we're glad you made it," he says as he leads me into his office.

Nervously, I make my way inside the splendid office. The view of the city from his window is just as breathtaking as it is from on the ground. I'm very impressed with Trinity already. I can tell the company takes care of its executives like they do their customers. *With an office this nice,* I think, *who would ever want to leave a company as prestigious as Trinity?*

After interviewing with Mr. Bedford for an hour, I'm given a tour of the office floor. I'm introduced to other employees while walking around, and am introduced as a possible future co-worker pending an offer. I'll certainly consider working for Trinity Corp. at any one of their Atlanta locations, especially if the price is right. I can live in Atlanta, but if an offer becomes available anywhere else, I'm willing to take that, too. Besides, right now, any new start will do.

Mr. Bedford's assistant Beverly asks me about what brings me to Atlanta. He informs her and the rest of the staff that I'm a victim of Hurricane Steven. Once the staff hears my story, they express their deepest sympathies. Some even attempt to give me money. The gesture's nice and thoughtful, but I tell them to call Ms. Stanley at the Red Cross if they want to help the neediest victims of Hurricane Steven. Although I can use the money, and I hope I didn't offend any of them by not taking it, I didn't think it was appropriate to accept it, considering how many other Hurricane Steven victims could use the money too.

Mr. Bedford tells me that Trinity Corp. has pledged to match, dollar for dollar, any money contributed by its employees to the Red Cross disaster fund, up to three million dollars. The contribution from Trinity Corp. will be a huge help.

Trinity Corp. isn't the only major donor. The city of Atlanta is also doing its part in a huge way. Atlanta has stepped in to offer aid to Hurricane Steven victims by donating the proceeds from a benefit concert it's sponsoring. Several Atlanta celebrities will participate. According to the local radio stations and news media, the concert is scheduled for the weekend of September the eighteenth at the Megaplex Arena. I'd love to go, but with who and how is the question. This concert would definitely ease my mind after all the recent stress and worry. Listening to something other than the news will take my mind off a lot of painful memories and hopefully ease the pain of Momma's death. But right now, I don't have a lot of money.

Besides, I'm taking it one day at a time right now, trying to get paper documents together in order to get assistance from FEMA and the Red Cross. So going to the concert is the last thing I can afford to spend money on when my bank account's getting low. But if I do get this job from Trinity, it couldn't come at a better time.

If I happen to get the job, I've decided I will donate ten percent of my earnings to the Red Cross to help in its effort to give aid to other disaster victims. It's the least I can do, after all they've been doing for me.

After the interview, I sit down in the nearby park to enjoy the fall afternoon scenery. I haven't seen a city so alive since New Orleans. The people of Atlanta are so friendly. As I haven't yet seen the city in its entirety, I decide to take a brisk walk down Peachtree Street. Exploring might take my mind off some of my worries.

Within minutes, I'm smiling from ear to ear. Just by walking normally, I'm noticed by nearly every man walking the street. Some whistle, while others speak to me or call out. Trying not to be unfriendly, I reply back. The little attention seems to lift up my spirits and restore my confidence as a woman. After so many days of depression, my confidence and my ability to feel beautiful seem to have taken a nosedive. I haven't felt pretty since the concert at the Mega Dome.

It feels good, getting the attention of a man for the first time in weeks. If only Christy and the girls were here with me, this would be one hell of an adventure. Especially with Kimberly, who absolutely loves nice-looking men. She would be in heaven. And Atlanta definitely has some good-looking men and some beautiful women.

As I'm standing in line at a street vendor to purchase some water, my eyes capture the attention of the cutest little girl. She's sitting in her stroller, and looks like she's at least one year old. It's obvious because her first two front teeth are just growing in. She is so adorable, with pigtails and the prettiest bright eyes. She's just grinning and smiling at me. I can't help but to smile back.

I lean over her to speak. "Hi," I say, smiling like a Cheshire cat. She smiles with all gums while lying back in her stroller. "How are you doing?" I ask. "You are *so* cute. What is your name?"

I straighten up and, like a breath of fresh air, her dad appears. My first thought is, *is this man gorgeous or what?*

"Hey, how are you doing?" he says in a sultry tone.

Looking at him very nervously, I reply, "Fine, and you?"

He gazes at me with his big brown eyes, looking like he was heaven-sent. "Just fine," he says. And is he ever!

[126]

"The name is Armstrong, Danny Armstrong. And this is my daughter, Brianna," he says, lifting her up and holding her in his arms. "And you are?"

Nervously, I shake his hand to introduce myself. "Angela Johnson," I say, blushing. No man has ever made me feel this way.

This is my kind of man, I think. He's about five foot ten with a muscular build. Well-groomed. Not too tall. Not too short. Just from looking at the definition of his muscles under his shirt, I can see he exercises regularly. He has the cutest baby face with an almond skin tone. My, do I like a good-looking man. I'm struck speechless just looking at him. Then he introduces himself and his daughter. Looking at her, I can tell there's no way he could deny her anything. She is so precious. And she looks just like him.

"So how's your day going?" he asks.

"So far so good," I say. I can even feel my blush reaching to my ears. "And yours?"

And with his masculine charm he replies, "It's much better, now that we've met."

Now, I've had men say the most flattering things to me. But I can't help but to smile, because it's the sweetest thing I've heard in a long time. Whether he's sincere or not, it feels good to hear. Though my stomach is filled with butterflies, I catch my composure and regroup.

"Is that so?" I say.

Danny looks into my eyes and says, "Yes," without a smirk or smile on his face.

"And why is that?" I question him.

He responds, "Because I've had a rough day. And to see a face as beautiful as yours aside from Brianna's makes my day worth living."

Dumbfounded by his unexpected kindness, I can feel myself get teary-eyed. "That's really sweet of you to say," I reply, trying to conceal my tears with a smile. "You know, I've had several rough days myself over the past few weeks. And meeting people like you often brightens my day and makes my day worth living, also," I say.

I smile at the same time he does, and suddenly I feel like laughing for the simple joy of it. After that brief moment together in Woodlawn Park, Danny and I become more acquainted. I tell him about my life, about moving here after Hurricane Steven, and he consoles me like a true friend.

We bond so well, it's like I've known him for years. I even became better acquainted with Brianna, who is the cutest. It feels good just being in the presence of Danny and Brianna. If God was to ever bless me with a husband and a child, Danny and Brianna would be perfect.

Chapter 12 - One Moment in Time

*S*eptember 20, 2004

*A*fter interviewing with Trinity two weeks ago, I have yet to receive a single phone call in reference to a job offer. But I'm still keeping my fingers crossed.

Since that lovely afternoon at Woodlawn Park in downtown Atlanta, Danny and I have met several times and spoken even more. I must say, he is a *very* sweet guy. And Brianna has stolen my heart. I never could've imagined I'd meet a man that could send chills through me the way Danny does. Just thinking about him makes me blush.

He has this personality that you can't help but to fall in love with. The type of personality that is so warm and caring that you just can't get enough of it. Danny and I have gone on two dates since we've met. One of the dates was nothing fancy, just an evening at a yogurt parlor. I had a Yogurt Bizarre, a chocolate cream yogurt with chocolate chip cookie dough and sprinkles. It was good. And Danny had a Strawberry Blast, a strawberry-pineapple smoothie with a power boost for energy. He let me taste some of it and it tasted pretty good. On our second date, we decided to go see an action movie called *The Hit*. I will say that, from start to finish, it was the best action-packed fall movie I've seen by far, though Danny's company might have had something to do with that.

After the movie, Danny surprised me by inviting me to the benefit concert Atlanta was sponsoring to raise money on behalf of Hurricane Steven victims. As a victim myself, I was touched by the city's overall initiative to help. The concert was really nice. We had the best seats in the house that money could buy. It was a wonderful evening, well worth remembering. And it was really sweet of Danny to invite me.

Afterward, we attended the after party at a club off Peachtree Street where Mayor Barbara Haywood was the honorary guest. The club was immaculately decorated and the crowd appeared to be mostly white-collar corporate business executives and political dignitaries. Some were the CEOs, owners, accountants, and CFOs of some of Atlanta's most prominent businesses. The company Danny keeps appears to feature some big movers. It makes me wonder what it is that he does for a living.

I'm not aware of just what he does at the company he works for, but he's a very busy man. He never mentions his work when we're together. He says his work time and his downtime are kept separated, that way he's able to enjoy Brianna and life without any of the worries of the office. He did tell me there was a time in his life when he rarely found time for himself or for anyone else. At times he was so busy he would eat, sleep, and breathe his job, with no time for distractions. But I see he found time to create that baby.

Because I, too, was once too busy for any distractions in my life, I can seriously relate to him. I can tell Danny must have one hell of a job. Each time we've been out on a date, his mobile phone never seemed to stop ringing. But out of respect for me, he never would answer the incoming call. I suppose that, because it was his downtime, he wouldn't answer the calls no matter who he was with. But I'd like to think that's not the only reason.

I must say, I admire this man and his work ethic. When a person such as Danny works that hard, they're usually trying to accomplish a major life goal. And looking at him, I think he has accomplished his goal. He is a very good man and a great parent, judging by what I've learned so far. And he's successful in whatever he does, because it shows in the confident way he handles his day-to-day business.

Because he's always humble, patient, and content with life, I can't imagine how his day could've been so rough when we met. We all have our days, and I guess that Monday when Danny and I met must've been 'one of those days' for him. But after we spent some time talking, it seemed his worries disappeared, if only for a brief moment. We were both in our own worlds where peace and tranquility were the only things on our minds. And we were there together.

Spending time with Danny and Brianna soothes my spirit. Whenever we're together, I feel so relaxed, almost like my world has frozen in time just for Danny Armstrong. Whenever we're together, I feel complete. And I've never met a man who has all the right characteristics and qualities I like, from the style of casual attire I prefer on a man to his sexy, masculine ways. And his overall demeanor is so charming that I can't help but fall head-over-heels for him.

What I admire more than anything is that he's a single parent. Now *this* is what really won me over. I've always dreamed of having a child where the father is around. Knowing that Danny is a family man gives me a sense of assurance that he will always make it a priority to be involved in his child's life. I know he wouldn't let our kids down if we were to have any. I don't know if I'm falling in love with him too soon, or if I am only infatuated with him, but I do know it feels good even to think about my future like this. It keeps my mind from thinking about Momma, Mark, and Christy.

Whenever Danny and I are together, he's such a perfect gentleman. He opens the door for me when entering a building or car, and he pulls my chair out for me during lunch or dinner. Whoever said chivalry was dead must not have known about Danny.

He and I have met for lunch twice this week at the Allison Building downtown. We would usually have a nice few moments alone to talk, and he has suggested that he'd rather discuss political and social issues instead of his job. He says concentrating on things in the outside world helps to take his mind off of the stress at work.

For some strange reason, he insists on taking care of me. But I tell him all the time I'm all right. I don't know if he's playing the sympathy card because I'm a hurricane victim and he looks good by trying to give me a handout. Or is he really so concerned about my tragic situation with Hurricane Steven that he just wants to be there for me? I'm at a loss for words because I'm not used to a man such as Danny being serious about wanting to take care of me.

It's nice and all, but I'd like to be there to take care of *him* when he's had a long day at work. He says just being in his company, I am. I don't know what more I can do, other than be there when he's had a long day at the office and just wants to lie in my arms and rest. I love it when he looks to me for affection. It feels so good to be needed.

Part of me is trying not to get too comfortable with him, because I may leave to go back to New Orleans someday soon. I know I'll be leaving, because I need closure before I can move on.

I need to see what's left of my beloved hometown. Whether I return to Atlanta will all depend on the condition of the city of New Orleans after the floods recede. I also need to know—if another hurricane like Steven were to hit

New Orleans, would the city be safe? Or would the levees break once more? Will the new levee systems be strong enough to prevent the waters of Lake Pontchartrain and the canals from overflowing into our neighborhoods? It's hard to determine. I need to return, to see the city with my own eyes, before I decide on anything permanent.

But Danny's been really helpful with guiding me through this tragic time in my life. He's such a sweet person. To help prove my identity as Angela Johnson rather than some random person, he helped to obtain my birth certificate from the Louisiana Department of Public Health. He also helped me locate Momma's body at the New Orleans city coroner so that I can identify and recover her body for burial. I don't know how he did it, but he did. I guess knowing the right people can get you what you're looking for. If I'd tried that on my own, I wouldn't have even known where to start, and I have no idea how long it would've taken me to get those much-needed items.

Somehow, despite his busy schedule and long hours at work, he even found the time to help me post a search notice on findalovedone.com for Mark and Christy. I'm not sure where Mark could be; I just know he was over at Dad's house the last time we spoke. And I know Christy was rescued days before me, but I don't know where she could be. Hopefully with the two of them posted on findalovedone.com I'll have some sort of luck in finding them or at least in learning what happened, if Mark was hurt or trapped in the storm. I just hope they both made it out safely. Danny reassures me that until I know otherwise, the most likely answer is that both Mark and Christy have found a place to stay somewhere. I hope so.

Danny's a mystery in some ways. I can tell that his everyday job is hectic, because he's constantly rushing to get back to the office for scheduled meetings. And coming home to care for a one-year-old child is another job in itself, but he's a true Mr. Mom. How does he do it? I have no idea. When I ask, he tells me that working and raising Brianna alone isn't easy. But he makes it appear effortless.

Whenever I'm visiting him, I try to ease some of the burden and tend to Brianna a little just so he can relax. Believe me, when I say that Brianna is a handful, she is, but I really don't mind. I've become deeply attached to her. And I can tell just from his facial expression that Danny's happy to have a break, even if it's for only a few minutes at a time. And it's obvious that having a woman's touch in the house is what's really needed to balance things out. But trust me, I'm not trying to get him too comfortable with the idea.

When I talk to Ms. Stanley about Danny, she reads me like Momma could whenever I was dating. Ms. Stanley tells me I am smitten; she can see it on my face. She knows Danny has touched my heart like no other man before him. I guess it's because of her motherly instincts that she's able to notice these things.

Just like a mother, she tells me all the time to be careful. I can tell she likes Danny because she's always asking me about him. But like a momma, she's also concerned, which I really do understand. I tell Ms. Stanley that Danny and I are just good friends so there's really no need to be concerned at all, but for some reason she shakes her head and smiles. Then she says, "Well, good friendships are what great relationships are built on."

And with a very wide smile I say, "Well, I do like Danny a lot. He's someone I'd love to have in my life someday as more than just good friends. But I'm not in a hurry."

"Well, if God's willing, He will see to it that you have that man to love and to hold, for better or for worse, until death do you part," Ms. Stanley replies. "Just have faith and be patient, baby."

Right now, faith is no concern at all. After waiting so long on Momma's rooftop for emergency crews to rescue me, my faith has gotten stronger.

My biggest concern is falling in love with Danny. That feeling is the one thing I haven't felt since dating Anthony after college. He was the only guy that truly swept me off my feet with his charms and boyish good looks. With Anthony, I just *knew* I was in love, and it broke my heart when we broke up. But I'm not sure where life is taking me right now. I've never really been in love with someone who cared for me as an equal. I've always kept myself busy trying not to love at all. And to fall in love with Danny only to go back to New Orleans will tear my heart to pieces. After all I've been through, I don't know if I can take any more pain.

I suppose that's why I'm holding my feelings back. But it's very hard not to become so close to Danny that I start to truly love him. He's all the man I've ever needed. He's kind, gentle, loyal, spiritually rooted, thoughtful, and very passionate about life. He says life is the most precious thing God gave to man, because God wanted man to become a living soul. And because of that gift, we must value the life we are given. His passion for life is easy to admire, and it makes me look at the world in new ways.

Danny and I have been talking for some time now, and the chemistry between us has gotten stronger. I think we would make a great couple. But loving him will make it difficult to go back to New Orleans, and that's where home is. But what's there to go back to? I have so many good memories of life there. I suppose holding onto the memories is what makes it so difficult to let go of the good times I had in New Orleans and accept that my home there is gone.

Will going back ease the pain from the devastation Steven caused? Will it help close this chapter of my life? Should I start anew and make a new life with Danny? I don't know, but what do I have to lose by going back to New Orleans in search of closure? Besides, I stand to gain a lot if it does help. Even though going back to New Orleans will surely be painful, if it can give my heart and soul some peace, the journey will have been worthwhile.

Getting a job offer at Trinity's corporate office in Atlanta will be a huge start in a new chapter. A job at Trinity will give me a foundation to build on, a place to start over in an entirely new city. Atlanta is nice, and I could be happy here. But if I were to receive an offer to work at one of Trinity's out-of-state offices, loving Danny will be complicated at best. I'm not too fond of long-distance relationships. They're difficult to maintain, and just thinking about it is painful already. But if we continue our friendship, I think the possibility of a relationship might be there.

Since I've come to Atlanta, Ms. Stanley and Danny have become like family to me. They've done so much to touch my heart in such a short time. Together, they've been by my side, giving me encouragement enough to lift my spirit up from the depths of depression. Between the two of them, they've managed to keep me busy, occupying my time and keeping my mind off of that tragic Fourth of July weekend.

Now that Ms. Stanley's aware that I worked at New Orleans City Hall as an administrative assistant, she has me volunteering my services to the Red Cross to help other victims of Hurricane Steven, a job which I find great pleasure in doing. And to put a little money in my pocket, Danny Armstrong, with his constantly busy schedule, has kindly asked if I could babysit Brianna for him on days when he has to fly in and out of town on company business to meet with potential clients.

After all we've shared together, I hate to leave the two of them behind in Atlanta just to go back to New Orleans. If I do decide to remain in New Orleans, I will still keep in contact with Danny and Ms. Stanley. I hope my friendship with them won't end once I leave. They are two wonderful people who I'll never forget, simply because of their kindness.

Chapter 13 - DMV Nightmare

*S*eptember 27, 2004

*I*t's been one hell of a week. I've been busy calling every DMV from Baton Rouge, Louisiana, to St. Charles, Louisiana, and back again to New Orleans, just to get some form of photo identification so I can have a Kinship DNA Analysis completed. That will let me recover Momma's body and verify that I'm the daughter of Ellyn Johnson. I've called every Department of Motor Vehicles that I was told to call and that might be able to help me.

After talking with the Louisiana DMV's branch manager in New Orleans, I'm told that the system that stores all the data is down due to a power failure and I should call the Baton Rouge location to see if I can retrieve my driver's license from that branch. I call them and come to find out they can't help me either. They say their system is down as well, also due to power failures caused by Hurricane Steven, and they have people working to restore the database and get the system back up and operating quickly. I am then transferred to the Department of Motor Vehicles branch in St. Charles, Louisiana, but the branch manager isn't able to help there either, due to the same power failure. I have to say, there's nothing quite as frustrating as being sent to 'a branch that can help' when that branch is shut down too. It has been more than two months since the hurricane struck. Surely by now, the DMVs should at least know which of their branches' databases are down from lack of power!

Anyway, although she is very helpful and cordial, the St. Charles branch manager informs me that the entire database for the Louisiana Department of Motor Vehicles is down. Just my luck, I guess. So, she gives me the number to the Department of Motor Vehicles in Arkansas. Why my driver's license would be in Arkansas is beyond me. Hesitant to call, I wait for a minute, hoping to ease my frustration. I thought getting my driver's license back was going to be simple, but it's becoming a nightmare.

I decide to call anyway just to hear what they'd have to say. And just like I figured, the Arkansas Department of Motor Vehicles wasn't much help at all, because it's an entirely different state, which I *knew*, but out of pure frustration and determination I called anyway. I was just hoping for some sort of answer. After several minutes of talking to the branch manager to figure out who else I can speak with that can help me get my driver's license, I'm told to call the New Orleans branch again. I called there earlier this week, but they were no help. No one seems to have any idea as to how long it will take to get the system restored and running again, so I end up calling almost every DMV in the state of Louisiana. Then, after calling back to the New Orleans branch, I'm placed on hold only to wait for the branch manager once again. All the while, I have to listen to some dreadful elevator music that's playing, which aggravates me even more.

However, this time I'm told that the DMV plans to release new driver's licenses and state identification cards to all residents. The branch manager tells me that the city of New Orleans is doing everything it possibly can, and as promptly as it can, to restore or replace its database. He says, "We've all been through a lot lately. Just be patient with us."

Then he continues, "The information will be made available in the next twenty-four hours. Residents will be able to browse the Louisiana Department of Motor Vehicles website, which will list instructions on how to obtain State Identification Cards and Driver's Licenses. We have been told that Governor Ashley Brown will issue a statement today via a press conference to announce further details on how to get proper identification from the website. We will soon be providing new State Identification Cards for all Hurricane Steven victims that need them."

At that point, frustrated with calling the Department of Motor Vehicles, I call it quits for the day.

I don't care how long it takes, really, although calling office after office only to be turned away is irritating. But I need my driver's license so I can take the Kinship DNA Analysis. I'm okay with waiting until tomorrow; I'm not in a hurry. But getting my driver's license will expedite the process for completing the DNA test, and I need to receive my results in order to recover Momma's body.

I'm told that a large percentage of the bodies that are being recovered from Hurricane Steven are badly decomposed. And there's no way to identify them without the DNA of a relative.

The New Orleans coroner tells me that I must have two forms of identification, such as a state-issued identification card or a driver's license, regardless of whether or not I have my birth certificate on hand. He says that it's part of their security protocol, and they absolutely must see two forms of identification. So I need a photo ID in addition to my birth certificate, which I already have. Then he tells me that Ellyn Johnson could be anyone's mother other than mine, which I understand. So to prove it, I must have a DNA test done.

Frustrated and tired from the day's ongoing problem of trying to get my driver's license, I fall asleep for a brief moment while waiting for Danny and Brianna to come home from work and daycare. Danny has kindly asked me to stay with him as an invited guest at his modest four-bedroom home in one of Atlanta's upscale suburban communities, and mentioned that I could sleep in the guestroom. I was very reluctant to stay with him at first. But after the Red Cross closed the housing center last week, I was left with nowhere else to go.

I'm emotionally torn. Danny and I have known one another for only a short period of time, and I feel that it's too soon for me to move in with him. But I do want to grace his presence every day. And moving in with him temporarily will give me the opportunity to do so.

After serious consideration and after talking it over with Ms. Stanley, I felt that it would be okay. She wished me luck and gave me her best regards. Although she has invited me to stay with her and Mr. Stanley in their lovely five-bedroom house in Midtown Atlanta, I just couldn't intrude upon their living space. They're very nice, but staying with Danny feels more like being with family.

Besides, after raising five children of their own, the Stanleys are well-established and recently retired. And I feel that having me around will hinder them from enjoying their retirement. Besides, their children have all grown up and moved out of the house to start families of their own. And I couldn't fill that extra bedroom space they left behind, because Momma used to tell me about how, when people are old enough to retire, they don't want to retire to children and grandchildren.

Remembering how I used to listen to Momma speak about retirement makes me very sure that Ms. Stanley and Mr. Stanley like to enjoy their living quarters.

Momma would always tell me that most retirees would like to retire in an appropriate way, where they're able to relax and enjoy the rest of their lives without dealing with children.

And Momma always said to me, many times, that when she became old enough to retire she would like to have Mark and me out of the house so she could enjoy her own space and peace of mind. And I'm sure Ms. Stanley and Mr. Stanley will be much the same. With me around, however temporarily, I'm sure I would take some of their peace of mind away.

Ms. Stanley and Mr. Stanley understand my concerns. Although they did ask that I stay, and said that it wouldn't be a problem if I chose to stay with them until I was able to get housing assistance from FEMA, they understand and respect my decision to stay with Danny. At least until I'm able to get back on my feet and move into my own apartment, which might be a while.

Trust me, I don't believe in 'playing house' with any man. If I'm going to live with a man and sleep in the same bed, it will be under the vows of marriage and not under the vows of friendship. Momma always told me to be careful if a man somehow can't ask me to marry him, but can ask me to come live with him instead. Is it a man who's just looking to have company? Someone he can entertain and call his wife at his leisure when guests are around? And when the guests have all left for the evening, am I just there to occupy space and add a woman's touch until the man decides whether he's ready for a commitment or ready for me to leave? She said I should know the answers before I move in.

I've always taken that one piece of advice seriously because Momma knew what was right for me. And because I'm Momma's only daughter, she wanted to make me aware of the motives some men have when they initiate that sort of move-in plan to women, such as entertaining her in exchange for her coming to occupy his space and keep him company.

So I made a vow to myself that I'm not moving in with anyone just to cook or clean his house. Personally, I don't think I should have to subject myself to the role of 'playing wife' to any man, let alone pretend to be a wife for a man's amusement. And I don't think any women should, either, but to each his own.

I've spoken with Danny about my views on living with him. Like a gentleman, he is very respectful of my feelings and he understands me clearly when I say I'm not going to be playing house or shacking up with him. He tells me he wouldn't put me in a position that will compromise my ethics. Nor would he place Brianna in a position that will compromise her feelings for me. He doesn't want just to have some fly-by-night relationship with a woman who becomes important in Brianna's life only to leave one day and never come back.

I have to say, his remark about Brianna hit me in the center of my heart and truly touched me. I know I'll be leaving Atlanta one day soon, and I may never return. But getting this emotionally attached to Brianna only to leave is something I don't want to do. I'd hate to get so close to her only to break her heart. I've gotten really attached to the other woman Danny loves so dearly. And she means a lot to me.

And with Danny raising Brianna on his own, she is in enough pain as it is now without her momma Sonya around to help. At her age, she just doesn't understand what she's feeling, but it's obvious that she feels something when her momma is so rarely there. I can see it in her eyes. I'm sure she can feel every bit of love I have for her in my heart because she smiles so brightly when I'm around. If only she knew how much her little smile makes my day?

Danny told me the story of Brianna's mother Sonya a few days ago. She wasn't ready to have a child. She felt that Brianna would jeopardize her advancement in the professional world as an aspiring model, and also keep her from achieving her goal of becoming a Senior Architect for Bobby Allison Properties one day.

When he told me, I thought, *now I've heard it all.* I'm not a mother as of yet, but when I do become one, I'll never use such a lame excuse to separate me from my child. What nerve! That sounded like one of the most selfish excuses a mother could have. Personally, I think she just wanted to continue enjoying life on her own without having the responsibility of a baby. Everyone has his or her reasons for not taking on a major responsibility such as raising a child, but *that* was just downright selfish. Remembering my brief moment with Megan, I feel a surge of sadness. I have to wonder how any mother could leave their child, under any circumstance.

Women have babies every day, I know. A friend of mine from college is now the Chief Operating Officer of Context Communications, Inc., a major wireless provider based in Phoenix, Arizona. With the help of her husband, who is a busy General Manager for CGN News, Beverly is raising her child without any problems. And her job's duties are to oversee the day-to-day operations of Context Communications, which provides wireless Internet service for the city of New Orleans. Surely her job is just as time-consuming as raising a child? But she manages. I'm aware of all this because I've seen Beverly juggle her career and family, describing in her letters to me how she and her husband find ways to do everything else and live, too.

Although her and her husband's careers are demanding, they decided there was really no excuse for either of them to up and leave their child alone to be cared for by one parent. That can-do attitude really matters. And from what I can see from the outside, they're doing a great job raising a family. I see, however, that Sonya felt otherwise.

So I don't think Sonya ever wanted the responsibility at all. Unless she's unfit or incapable of raising Brianna, no woman in her right mind would give up a child that precious. And Sonya is neither unfit nor incapable. Her lifestyle is just, in her own opinion, too demanding to leave room for a little girl.

Danny tells me she's a prominent figure in the world of modeling. And because of her busy schedule, she's told him on several occasions that she'll never have time to love and care for Brianna the way she deserves. Although he doesn't speak ill of her, I can't help but think, *what a lame excuse for a mom.* But in spite of his busy schedule, Danny quickly took the initiative to get full custody to raise Brianna. Now *that*'s a man who's taking care of his priorities and dealing with his responsibilities in a mature way.

And it's all part of why I care about him so much. He's so different from many of the guys I knew living in the Lower 9th Ward, who didn't bother to care for their children, sometimes because they weren't even responsible enough to care for themselves. Danny is one of the few men I know that does.

Only God knows what Danny goes through daily. I'm not entirely sure, only because he hasn't mentioned the exact kind of work he does. I just know he's always busy, doing God knows what. But he doesn't seem to mind. His feelings about Brianna are obvious; you can see the love in his eyes whenever he sees her face.

I will do my best to be supportive of him and to help with Brianna as often as I can. I have to admit, though, the fact that Brianna has touched my heart in a deep way only makes leaving harder.

Chapter 14 - Day of Reckoning

*O*ctober 5, 2004

*T*he day has finally come when I can take the Kinship DNA Analysis, the test which will let me properly identify Momma's body and prove that Ellyn Johnson is my momma so I can see that she's buried properly. God knows I've waited long enough for this day to come; I'm so ready to get it over with. The nurse tells me that it will be a quick procedure. I don't know what to expect.

I've waited patiently for four days to receive my driver's license from the New Orleans Department of Motor Vehicles so I can have this done. Browsing the New Orleans DMV website, I was instructed to locate the city and state I'm currently living in and then request to have my driver's license transferred to the nearest Department of Motor Vehicles branch, which is located in Atlanta. I was able to pick up both it and my state ID card at the downtown branch yesterday.

I could've had them mailed to Danny's house, of course. However, if I had done that, the process could have taken a month due to the overwhelming requests for driver's licenses and state identification cards from former New Orleans residents. The New Orleans branch manager said it normally took seven to ten days to process and mail requests, but with so many requests coming in at once, it might take much longer.

However, thanks to Mr. Thompson, our New Orleans city councilman and district representative for the Lower 9th Ward, some of the residents from his district were able to have their driver's licenses sent electronically to the nearest DMV. I was fortunate to have my driver's license electronically mailed, because it took four days for me to get it compared to a month. I'm so glad about that. I need to get the DNA test done to recover Momma's body and to file a claim with her insurance company.

Now that I have a valid identification card, my life feels more complete. I can hardly wait until I'm able to prove to the insurance company that I am Angela Johnson. I really think that having Momma buried properly and respectfully will give me some closure and help me to move on in my life.

It's been a struggle. Even though I had my birth certificate, I still wasn't able to prove that I am the same Angela Johnson it says I am on my birth certificate. Trust me, walking around with just a piece of paper and trying to prove to other people who you are requires a lot of explaining and a lot of headaches, especially when they're the people trying to help you.

I'm not the only one who has had to deal with this. Many New Orleans evacuees have gotten frustrated with the government and many of the non-profit organizations like the Red Cross and the Give a Hand Foundation which are helping to find housing and employment for them. Due to all of the red tape and security protocols, it's been difficult for anyone without the proper identification to receive any financial, medical, employment or housing assistance.

The situation is unusually bad because many of the people who were evacuated in a hurry left New Orleans without any money or identification in their pockets. While some are blessed to have family and friends in metro Atlanta who they can stay with, others were still waiting to receive assistance when the shelters were closed down last week. Now, some of them are living in homeless shelters now while they wait for DNA tests and backlogged ID requests to go through. It's a mess.

I can understand why the government mandates that any New Orleans resident seeking government assistance must have some form of picture identification verifying that they lived in the New Orleans area. But why do we have to go through so much red tape to get identification in the first place? If nothing else, this whole experience has shown me how lucky I was. I had one form of ID, which made it easier to prove who I am. I can hardly imagine what it must be like for the people who lost everything to the hurricane only to end up in a homeless shelter in a city far away from home.

After these past several months of no longer working for the New Orleans City Hall, my checking and saving accounts are now depleted. And money is harder than ever to come by. Even with the money Danny pays me for babysitting Brianna, I can barely afford to buy a new wardrobe to wear so I can dress appropriately if Trinity Corp. decides to hire me. And getting a job isn't as easy as it might appear due to the economy. Unemployment is at its highest in six years. Some sixty thousand Americans have lost their jobs due to Hurricane Steven. And with credit stipulations and lack of education, getting a job will be even more complicated for a lot of evacuees because a lot of them don't have credit at all or have abused it entirely too much. The cost of living is up and hourly wages don't ever seem to be enough to make ends meet. It's bad enough that some say we are headed for a recession. Hell, every day is a recession for me and for my fellow evacuees.

In my opinion, employers are asking for entirely too much just to get paid a minimum hourly wage. It's hard for many people out here to make a living. But I don't think employers really care. To them, it's all numbers. Honestly, though, what does credit have to do with anyone getting a job? I've been told that employers use credit to judge the character of the person applying. But at a time like this, many hurricane victims are using their credit cards to try to pull them through until they can get a job, and that can quickly lower your credit. I can only hope and pray that Trinity will look at my work ethics and my experience, not my credit score. Because like many evacuees and many Americans alike, my credit isn't superb, only fair. I'll just keep my fingers crossed and hope that God will bless me with the job, because right now I sure could use it.

Having spent two hundred dollars I didn't anticipate over the course of a week for food and the bare necessities, I'm down to my last twenty dollars. I don't know how far twenty dollars will take me, and I may have to get a loan from Ms. Stanley. This is something I hate doing because I don't feel that I know her well enough to ask to borrow money. But she's been there for me like a mom and has always told me, "If you need anything, let me know." So it can't hurt to ask.

At least I feel more comfortable about asking her than I do about asking Danny. I don't think he'd mind, but I can't ask—my pride just won't let me. Besides, he's being a great help already by allowing me to stay in his guestroom.

Fortunately, I'm not looking to borrow much, just enough to sustain me until FEMA approves my financial aid. According to Ms. Stanley, I should be approved the same day I apply, assuming that I am able to verify my last place of residency. Now that I have two forms of identification, I can.

However, Ms. Stanley tells me that FEMA is giving out three thousand dollar prepaid debit cards to help evacuees get back on their feet, and they're hoping the money goes to good use. She says that, according to the news, President Riley asked Congress for fifteen billion dollars in emergency funds to give to FEMA. The money is to be distributed to help New Orleans pay for cleanup and recovery expenses as well as to support evacuees with monetary needs. That sounds very helpful for many Hurricane Steven victims, including myself.

#

After several minutes in the medical office, I'm given a quick swab on the inner cheek of my mouth with a Q-tip and then I'm released, just like that. I thought maybe it would be a long and painful process, like a finger prick or some type of blood transfusion, but it wasn't. I have to admit, I was a little nervous. The DNA specialist recommended by the Find Family National Call Center tells me my results should be returned to me in maybe a month or two.

Chapter 15 - Getting to Know All About You

*O*ctober 17, 2004

*A*utumn is in the air. The fall foliage has begun its seasonal change. Leaves of brown, red, and orange have fallen from the trees, and pine cones cover the ground to sow a new harvest of pine trees for springtime. The weather feels nice and brisk on this cool Sunday afternoon. Danny, Brianna, and I are participating in the annual AIDS Walk in Dearborn Park, along with hundreds of local high school and college students, churchgoers, and employees of retail businesses and eateries as well as advertising and financial firms.

The walk is three miles long, which will give Danny and me plenty of much needed time to talk a little more about our future, be it together or not.

I don't want to frighten him and speak too soon about a committed relationship, but I would like to know about his plans for his future, and if there's any room for a nice woman like me in it.

He's the Jamal Davenport I've waited for to come sweep me off my feet. And he truly has. I've never met a man like Danny, one that's so passionate about life, one who would donate his last dime or give away his last meal to help others in need. And he doesn't expect anything in return for his charity.

He told me several days ago that he's a major contributor to the AIDS Walk and that he does the walk each year. He invited me to come along with him and Brianna to this year's so that we can spend some quality time together, an offer which I was glad to accept. What better way to spend my Sunday than by giving my time to a worthy cause such as the fight to cure AIDS? I'm not walking just to impress Danny or showing him I'm interested just because he does this walk each year. I do care about the cause. And it's nice to know that he does, too.

While we're waiting for the walk to start at the south entrance of the park near the corner of Piedmont Road and Monroe Drive, we are greeted by fifteen of Danny's co-workers, who proudly wear illustrated T-shirts displaying a graphic logo of Armstrong Marketing.

I look closely at the logo. It looks familiar. I've seen the logo somewhere before, but where? Curious as to where I've seen the illustration of Armstrong Marketing, I ask Danny jokingly, "So, do I get a T-shirt with your name on it?"

Without hesitation, he replies, "Sure," takes an extra T-shirt from Brianna's stroller, and hands it to me. Very seriously, he says, "My reason for inviting you today was not only to let me spend quality time with you and walk in the AIDS Walk, but also to welcome you into the world of Danny Armstrong, where every day is a rough day for me. Especially being the owner and CEO of one of Atlanta's largest African American marketing firms."

After a second, closer observation of the Armstrong Marketing logo, I can remember seeing it on the directory of the Allison Building in downtown Atlanta when I went for my job interview with Trinity Corp. As I recall, Armstrong Marketing takes up the entire forty-fourth floor.

Standing in the middle of his employees, I put the T-shirt on, and Danny continues to tell me more about his company. He says Armstrong Marketing has a staff of thirty employees with a projected revenue of eight million dollars a year. Established in 2001, the company holds several major contracts with prominent clients in sports, music, wireless communication, and non-profit organizations, such as the Miami Blue Fins, Atlantis Records, and my friend Beverly's company, Context Communications, Inc. He says providing his marketing services to charitable organizations like the AIDS Walk is just one of the ways he gives back to the community. I must admit, I'm very impressed.

We start the three-mile walk. I try to act casual, as if the man I'm falling in love with hadn't just told me that he not only works hard to be a good father, but also runs his own company. I have no idea how he manages, but I'm even more impressed than before.

"Wow," I say finally. "All this time, I thought you were just some busy junior executive for an advertising firm. I never would've thought you were the Chief Executive Officer of the firm," I say, waving at the homeowners standing in their front yards watching the AIDS Walk. "So this is what you do for a living?"

"Yeah, this is my life, walking the AIDS Walk," Danny says, laughing.

I give Danny a slight nudge on the shoulder, "No, silly. You know what I'm saying."

He laughs and replies, "Oh, you meant is marketing what I do for a living, my bad."

I roll my eyes at him jokingly. "You make me sick," I say, laughing, but with a bit of an attitude. "And how long have you been pursuing this dream of owning your own business, mister smart butt? And what made you pursue marketing?"

Danny's laughing, and has to take a moment to catch his breath. Finally Danny replies, "I'm sorry, but I had to," and he laughs again.

"Whatever," I say, smiling too.

"No, really. I've had a dream of running my own business ever since I was a child," he says, more seriously. "Growing up, I would watch my mom and dad put in so much time and energy fulfilling someone else's dream, only to make that person and their company successful. So I made a promise to myself that if I ever worked myself that hard, I would do it for no one but myself, so I started a business and that's what I did."

"And your niche was marketing?"

"Actually, marketing was my major at Julian University in Seattle, Washington. My niche is business." He says it flatly, not bragging, and without any notion of arrogance. "I just incorporated the two during my internship at Atlantis Records."

"You were an intern at Atlantis Records?" I ask, surprised. "And you have a contract to do the marketing for the same company?"

"Yeah," he says. "I helped launch the marketing campaigns that propelled R&B sensation Ms. Nichole and the all-male band Momentum into their music careers." Danny calmly adds, "I knew from there I was onto something big.

"So," he continues, "instead of accepting the Senior Marketing Director position Atlantis offered, I decided to take my network and start my own marketing firm. And that's how Armstrong Marketing began, a little over two years ago."

"Wow," I say. "That's amazing. And it's a little funny, because I just saw Ms. Nicole and Momentum perform during the Fourth of July Music Festival in New Orleans."

"Yeah," Danny says, nodding. "I was scheduled to attend that show, but I had to hold a last-minute meeting with the record company that weekend to discuss a new R&B project they're looking to release this fall." He shakes his head. "It's sad to know that Hurricane Steven hit during the same time."

"Yeah, I just hope everyone that could've gotten out of New Orleans that day was able to," I say sadly. But I'm getting better at dealing with my loss, and quickly move to another topic. "Not to change the subject, but how did you like the music industry?" I ask, genuinely curious.

"It was nice to me," Danny says, then more quietly repeats, "it was nice to me." And without another word, he stops talking. And for the rest of the walk, he doesn't mention anything else about his career in the music industry.

Gracefully we walk up Piedmont Road together, where several AIDS Walk volunteers and an Atlanta Police Officer, all of whom appear to be enjoying their afternoon, stop everyone at a red light so the afternoon traffic can pass by. Looking at the overall crowd, it seems everyone there is excited to be walking. A fairly large percentage of the participants are walking with their gay lovers. It's a beautiful sight to see how times have changed. And how people have come out, having nothing to hide any more about their sexual preferences.

Everywhere I turn, I see lovely couples out enjoying themselves. The AIDS Walk has given them the freedom to be who they are and to express themselves more freely. And they've come out in force to help in the fight against AIDS.

Danny informs me about the turnout from the gay community and how supportive they are. However, I honestly never expected to see so many at one time. He told me days ago that if I would be uncomfortable, I didn't have to attend. But because my friend Tasha is bisexual, I don't see anything wrong with the lifestyle. As I always say, to each his own.

In New Orleans, it would truly be a sight to see so many homosexuals together at one time and place. During Mardi Gras, you'll see a few here and there, having a good time dressed as women or just having fun with their significant other. Every now and then, you might see a couple walking together in the city, but nothing of this magnitude.

Besides, New Orleans's gay community isn't as big as Atlanta's, judging from what I can see. Some of the people living in New Orleans find it hard to accept the lifestyle. I couldn't tell you why, but it's an ongoing issue. Rival gang members taunt and physically abuse homosexuals. I firmly believe anyone caught in the act of gay bashing should be punished to the full extent of the law and prosecuted, but still, the harassment continues.

We pass the halfway point, then the two-mile marker. The walk isn't bad. I'm not as tired as I thought I'd be; actually, it feels really good to get out in the fresh air and to see all the autumn colors. Although we and the other people participating in the walk are walking in the middle of Peachtree Street and have to move slowly so oncoming traffic can go past, Danny and I are making great progress with Brianna resting contentedly in her stroller.

I'm still interested in knowing more about Danny Armstrong's future plans, goals, and dreams, so I engage him in more conversation.

"Now that you've accomplished your dream, what's next for you?" I ask.

Danny looks at me and smiles. "I'm not sure," Danny says, "but wherever God leads me, I hope I'm prepared for the challenge."

"You will be," I say confidently. "God will prepare you for what's next in your life when He knows you have mastered the challenge He's put before you already."

Danny's smile turns into a grin. "Well, so far so good. I've conquered every challenge God has put before me except marriage," Danny says, then blushes. "That may be the biggest challenge of all."

"And when that time comes, God will prepare you for it," I say.

"Well, from the look of things, I think I'm ready," he says. "I'm blessed to have all I need. I have a successful business with a great staff, good friends, and a lovely daughter. What more can a man ask for, besides a great wife?"

One thing I've noticed about Danny is that he rarely if ever speaks about the material things God's blessed him with. He's such a modest and humble man, and he appreciates the value of family and friends so much that in comparison, material things have no value in his life at all.

With a quiet laugh, I ask, "Well, would you like to get married some day?"

"I would. What about you?" he asks.

"That's a dream I'd like to accomplish," I say. I pause, taking a moment of silence. Then I go on. "I promised my Momma before she passed that I'd get married and have grandkids one day for her."

"And you will," Danny says. "God may be getting you prepared for the right man."

"Well, when you see him, let me know," I say, smiling at Danny.

"I will. Who knows," he says, a little mischievously, "he may be right under your nose."

I chuckled. "Well, I wish he'd make himself known."

"He may already have," Danny says.

And with a slight blush, I reply, "Well, I don't see him."

Danny looks at me, bringing Brianna's stroller carefully to a stop. His eyes are bright with burning passion. "You may be looking right at him," he says with his sultry voice.

"Is that so?" I ask, looking into his eyes.

"Yeah," Danny says as he make eye contact.

"And what does my future hold with this man?" I ask.

"A lifetime of everlasting bliss is what's waiting," Danny promises. "I'll see to it that a woman as precious as you doesn't have to hurt any more or worry about a thing. And I'll ease every pain in your body."

Those are the last words I hear as we approach the end of the AIDS Walk. Everything else he says fades into the background, and I can't recall anything after that. At this moment, time stands still, and a vision of Danny and me happily married fills my mind. I know, at this instant, that he's the man I've prayed for. And all the time, he *has* been standing right under my nose.

Chapter 16 - Truth Revealed

November 17, 2004

"Hello," the voice says over the phone. "May I speak to Angela Johnson?"

"This is she," I say.

"This is Nancy Ferrymen calling from Dr. Brooke's office. How are you doing today?" she asks.

"Just fine, thanks."

"I was calling to let you know that your DNA results have come in. And as of Tuesday morning, I have express-delivered them over to the State Police Crime Laboratory. You may want to call the laboratory to verify that they have received it. And I hope you're able to take care of everything with the insurance company."

"Thank you," I say.

"If the insurance company needs more information, they may contact me at the office and I'll be glad to send it to them," she says.

"Okay."

"Well, thank you for allowing us to perform this service for you. And if there's anything else we can do to be of help, please feel free to give us a call," she says.

"I will. And thank you so much," I say sincerely.

Excited about the news of my DNA results, I call the State Police Crime Lab to verify that they've received the results. After several minutes of waiting on the phone, someone finally answers.

"Louisiana State Police Crime Lab, Pauline speaking. How may I help you?" she asks in a deep Louisianan accent.

"My name is Angela Johnson. I'm calling in reference to a DNA test result that was Express delivered to your office Tuesday morning from Dr. Brooke's office in Atlanta," I say.

"Okay, and your name again, sweetie?"

"Angela, Angela Johnson."

"Okay, hold on for a split-second sweetie, and let me look through our incoming mail." I can hear Pauline sifting through papers as I wait on the phone. Although it's only a few seconds of waiting, my excitement makes it feel like minutes are going by.

"Okay sweetie, Angela Johnson," she confirms. "Yes, we received the results yesterday morning."

"Oh great. So what should I do from here?" I ask.

There's a brief moment of silence before she replies. "If I'm correct, is this pertaining to the deceased victim Ellyn M. Johnson?" she asks.

"Yes. She's my mother."

Pauline takes a sudden deep breath and exhales slowly.

"We've been waiting to send your results over to the State Medical Examiner so the remains can be identified. However, after careful comparison with your DNA, we've discovered that Ellyn Johnson is not your biological mother. Therefore, we can't proceed any further."

My entire body goes numb from shock and I fall speechless. I can't believe this. This can't be true. The results must have been mistaken. Did I really hear what I thought I just heard?

"Are you sure?" I ask frantically.

"Yes," Pauline says. "I'm sorry, sweetie. In cases like these, we carefully check and double-check to be sure. But yes, those are the results."

"But ... how could that be?" I ask, my throat suddenly choking up as I try not to cry.

"Well, we examined the family reference samples provided by you and by Ellyn Johnson's known family members. Using those samples, we were unable to determine a probable relationship between you and Ellyn Johnson or any of Ellyn Johnson's known family. Therefore, the probability of you being related to Ellyn Johnson is extremely small—much less likely than one in a million. Simply put, the DNA samples we have on record from you and from Ellyn Johnson don't match."

Though I'm caught by surprise, I quickly respond. "So, what are you saying?" I'm trying to gather my thoughts without being hesitant. "I don't think I heard you well, do you mind repeating that?"

"I'm sorry, Ms. Johnson," Pauline says, "but Ellyn Johnson is not your mother."

"Oh God, no," I say. The lump in my throat is huge now, and I find myself starting to cry uncontrollably as my already-shaken world falls apart.

Pauline waits for me to recover. "I'm sorry. I'm so sorry," she says. There is such empathy in her voice. I don't know what I would do if she had just hung up the phone on me.

I get a hold of myself. Sniffling, I start to ramble, desperate for answers. "So how can I see her? I mean, who should I talk to? You said something about other family members. Who else was it that gave DNA besides me?"

"I'm sorry, Ms. Johnson, but I'm not able to disclose that information. According to our database, there were four other family members who came forward in the past month to contribute reference samples to help build a genetic family tree for Ellyn M. Johnson," she says.

Four other family members, I repeat to myself. I wonder who they were. Could one of them have been Mark? If so, he's alive. But the DNA samples could have come from any four of Momma's siblings.

"Is there anyone I can speak to that will let me see her?" I ask.

"It's possible," she says. She pauses. "Let me think. Yes, you can contact the State Medical Examiner, Dr. Steven Barton, who's handling the identification of all remains recovered from the area affected by Hurricane Steven," Pauline tells me. "The body has been prepared for release and identification as of a week ago. So when you're able to, you may come view her body at any time. But I must warn you that Dr. Barton isn't going to release Ms. Johnson to you without a probable positive identification."

Slowly, I place the phone into its cradle and collapse into a nearby chair. I cry my heart out. Nonstop tears run from my eyes. "This can't be true!" I scream to the empty house. "Oh my God," I say more quietly, gulping for air between sobs. "This can't be true. Oh, God, no," I cry.

I don't know what to think anymore. Ellyn Johnson has been my momma my entire life. And she will forever be; no DNA test can change the love she gave me. But why didn't she tell me about this? Why did I have to find out this way? I need to take a closer look at my birth certificate. I hope I can find some answers there.

Trying to gather myself together, I walk around Danny's house from one room to another in a kind of daze. At times I feel almost weak enough to pass out, and I have to stop for a while to sort through my thoughts at the dining room table. Even just sitting here, the pain is so intense, I can barely breathe.

It's been well over four months now since Momma's death. I was looking forward to the opportunity to see her one last time. But knowing she's not my biological mother, I don't know if I can take this. Since she isn't, then who is? I would at least like to know that much.

I knew the day would come for me to view her body and see her laid to rest. But never in my life did I expect the day would come that I'd discover Ellyn Johnson isn't my biological mother. Pacing around the house, I plead to God for answers. Why did He have to take her? Why did all of this have to happen to me? Did Mark and Daddy make it out of New Orleans safe and sound, or did they pass in the storm too? With so many emotions running through me, I wonder if Mark is my biological brother. Am I adopted? I ask myself. Or was there an error at the hospital? Is Momma's real daughter living her own life somewhere, blissfully unaware that the family she grew up in isn't actually related to her?

So many questions, and no answers. Not today.

At last, the ripped feeling in my heart eases a little and the sobs die away. Finally, I wipe away my tears and walk into the family room to sit down on the couch and gather my thoughts. I have no idea how I am going to handle all this. This is going to be the hardest thing I've ever done in my entire life. I knew it was going to be hard to bury Momma, but burying the mother I've known my entire life, only to find out that she isn't really my mother, is going to be a hundred times harder. God knows, I may end up burying my entire family.

The last thought alone hits me like a mallet. I lie down on the sofa, curl up into the fetal position, and cry.

This time, when the tears stop, I feel empty inside, but better. Almost relieved. Somehow, I've survived everything life and God have thrown at me. I don't know that I'm stronger now than I was then, but I've endured. Somehow.

I think about my family. Momma, Mark, and Daddy. I can't imagine life without them. I've been living without any of them for four months, and it's been slowly eating at me. Less than an hour ago, when I got the news that Momma wasn't my biological mother, I felt as though my heart had been torn apart.

But every day, I think of her. The things she did, the advice she gave. Her lessons about life, love, and faith. Every day, I pray for her, hoping that God will keep her as He has her entire life, close to my heart and to His. I don't know what I am going to do now, but even if the worst has happened and I never see Mark or Daddy again, I know I will somehow keep going. They will live on in my heart, if nowhere else.

As I raise myself into a sitting position, I let memories of Momma flood through me. Tears of joy and laughter flow down my face. I can't help but to smile.

She had this bad habit of playing with her hair whenever she was thinking. I remember one time, several months before the storm, when Christy and I invited her to have lunch with us at Jackson Square. Mr. Thompson joined us and started telling us about his plans for the 9th Ward district. None of us had expected to hear about that, but we were too polite to interrupt, and he went on talking anyway. He planned to redevelop the poverty-stricken areas of the Lower 9th Ward and establish an "Empowerment Zone," a place where certain areas would receive government aid and be developed into newly renovated houses, subsidized apartments, and strip malls to improve the community's infrastructure.

Because Momma knew redeveloping the Lower 9th Ward required it being torn down first, she didn't care to listen to Mr. Thompson and his plans. Oh, she knew it wasn't likely to happen any time soon because it hadn't happened since she's lived in the Lower 9th Ward, and that's been a good few decades. Besides, Mr. Thompson has been talking about redeveloping the 9th Ward ever since I've been working at City Hall—three years, at that point. I suppose it's sadly ironic that he tried for years to start tearing down parts of the Lower 9th Ward so they could be redeveloped, and then some random hurricane came along and tore the district up for him.

In any case, Momma knew that Mr. Thompson was talking so much hot air. So instead of listening, she just nodded and um-hmm'd whenever Mr. Thompson seemed to expect it, and used the time for thinking instead.

And all the while Mr. Thompson was talking, Momma was playing with the ends of her nice long hair. I knew she was thinking about something, but what? When I asked, she said she'd tell me when we got home, but never did. Later, when I reminded her, she told me she still wasn't ready to tell me. Now I wonder whether she was going to tell me the story behind why she isn't my biological mother. I guess I'll never know.

I really need to talk this over with someone. Danny's at work, so I decide to call Ms. Stanley first. With the Red Cross housing center closed, I haven't been able to speak with Ms. Stanley as often as I have before, so I have to call her at home and bother her. I don't like doing that, but I really need her advice. "Hi, Ms. Stanley," I say when she picks up.

"Hey baby, how are you doing?" she asks excitedly. "How's everything?"

"Okay, for the most part," I say somberly.

"That's good, that's real good baby."

"I got my DNA test results back today," I say. I'm starting to cry again, but not so badly as before. "I found out that Ellyn Johnson isn't my biological mother."

"Oh baby," Ms. Stanley says. I can feel the sympathy in her voice even over the phone. "Are you sure?"

"Yes."

"Oh Angela, I'm so sorry to hear that," she says. "Well, regardless of what those people might have said, if you know in your heart that Ellyn Johnson is your mother, then child, don't let some DNA test change the way you feel about her." Like a concerned mother, she adds, "Now you go ahead and handle your business like your momma would like for you too, baby. Don't let this break your spirit, okay?"

"Okay," I say. Her warm words and obvious concern are incredibly comforting.

"You get on with your life and make your momma proud of you. You keep your head up, because God is going to see you through this, you hear?" Ms. Stanley says.

"Yes," I assure her. "I will."

"Now let's get them tears from your eyes. I know it hurts, honey, but you got to keep moving. If you stop, you will never make it to where God needs you to go, okay? Like I've told you before, I'm here whenever you need me. Now, I may not be your mother, child, but I've come to love you like one of my own." My heart swells at the emotion in her words.

"And if you ever need anything, I'm here, baby," Ms. Stanley says. "If you need to stop by the house, you know the door's always open for you, okay?"

"Yes," I say, sniffling. "Thank you."

And with great concern in her voice, she replies, "All right, now. Wipe away those tears for me, okay, baby? It's gon' be all right. I know you're hurting, but you've got to stay strong."

"Okay," I say. I find a napkin and wipe the tears from my eyes.

"Now you go ahead and handle your business. If you need me I'm here, okay?"

"Okay," I whisper.

"All right, I'll talk to you later, okay?" she says.

I sniff back a few stray tears and I reply, "Okay, bye."

"Bye-bye, sweetie."

And like a mother, her love soothes my soul. Suddenly, I'm feeling a lot better. I know I'm still a little emotional, so I take time alone to gather my thoughts. I need to make plans for travel arrangements, first of all, so I can see Momma and say my final goodbyes. I need to let Danny know that I'm leaving. And some time in the next few days, I need to make a decision: should I return to New Orleans or stay here in Atlanta? Nearly everything else can wait.

Whether I return depends on so many things. Can I get my job back at City Hall, if City Hall is still running? Can I find a place to live?

And just as important, am I willing to lose the things I have here? I've met a nice man who makes me feel like a queen. And I have a chance of getting a nice job with a great company. Is it worth giving up all of this, after I've lost so much already?

After I've had several hours to sit and think things over, Danny arrives home with Brianna, who he has just picked up from daycare. Since I've been living here for the past few weeks, Danny casually walks over and greets me with a hug like he always does.

"So how are you doing?" Danny asks.

"I could be better," I say, sighing.

"Okay, talk to me. What's going on?" he asks.

And before I can say a word, I fall into his arms and hug him fiercely.

"Okay," Danny says, holding me tightly. "It's okay, it's okay."

He holds me close to his chest as my tears run down his silk tie and Oxford polo shirt. "All right, all right, it's okay, it's okay," he says. He rubs his hands up and down my back. He lets me bury my head in his manly chest, and then leans forward a little and kisses my forehead.

Suddenly he holds me up away from his chest, and helps me steady myself. "Okay, you're going to have to talk to me. Tell me what's going on," he says gently. "That is the only way I can help you."

With a handful of tissues ready, I sit down on the couch while Danny removes Brianna from her stroller. Holding a tissue firmly, I wipe the tears from my eyes.

I say, "Dr. Brooke's receptionist called me today. My DNA results came in," I say, looking at the tissue. It's easier to focus on something small instead of trying to look a friend like Danny in the face.

"That's great, isn't it? Now you can recover your momma's body and take care of the insurance claim,"

Danny says. He's smiling, happy for me, but I can see he's concerned.

And the thought of what might have been sends fresh tears to my eyes and makes me break down crying. And Danny, ever the gentleman, stands by my side to comfort me.

"Okay," he soothes me. "Just take your time. I have all night. I'm going to get Brianna ready for bed now, so when you're ready to talk, just let me know. I'm here."

Graciously, he takes Brianna by the hand and together they walk into the kitchen to put away her bottles. I watch them as I sort through my thoughts. It's comforting just to see them together. I watch as Brianna takes careful step after careful step, clutching her father's hand. The warm moment is the highlight of my day.

After sitting there for a moment, I get up and walk into the kitchen. With an island big enough to feature a kitchen sink, dishwasher, and a cooking range in the center of the room, Danny's kitchen is as spacious as the kitchen at Ricky's house that I once thought so amazing.

Smiling from ear to ear at the sight of Brianna reaching for me, I pick up Brianna, who smiles back at me, all teeth and gums. I give her a kiss on the cheek and set her down again. She moves away for a moment, looking around, and then, turning, she runs up to me in the spacious kitchen with open arms outstretched so I can pick her up and hold her. And for the first time today, I laugh in delight.

Danny comes over to place his strong arms around us.

"So, are you feeling better?" he asks.

"Not really," I say, somber again. "The DNA results came back proving that Ellyn Johnson is not my mother."

"Oh Angela," he says, "I'm sorry to hear it. Are they sure?"

"Yes," I say sadly.

Danny steps away, turning to face me as he leans up against the kitchen island. He looks especially thoughtful.

"Wow," he says. "This just can't be real. After all these years, you mean to tell me your momma never told you?"

"No, never. I believe she was thinking about how to tell me several months ago, but she never got around to it."

Danny nods. "So when are you going back to New Orleans to view and recover the body?"

"I'm not sure," I say honestly. I pause, thinking to myself. "Maybe this Saturday. I have to go find out when the funeral is."

After a little more discussion about going back to New Orleans, Danny and I put Brianna to bed. *Is this not the family I've longed for?* I ask myself, feeling guilty that I might soon be leaving them forever. What a wonderful way to start over, if I stay. I know it will be difficult to make that choice, but the only thing left to do is to go back. New Orleans is where I call home and it's where I left my heart: Momma. I definitely need closure. Then, and only then, will I know for sure where I belong.

I pause in the middle of what I'm doing. Suddenly, I realize that I haven't really been comparing the options. Instead, I've been trying to convince myself to let go of New Orleans, at least enough to allow me to stay here with Danny and Brianna.

That thought makes my heart feel lighter. I consider the past few days, and yes, I think it's true. I've made up my mind that New Orleans isn't where I belong anymore.

It will always be important to me, and it will always be my hometown, the place that helped to shape me into the person I am. But I've come to realize that when God allows something in our lives to come to an end, He does it knowing that we are strong enough to go on to the next challenge, the next adventure.

I haven't defeated New Orleans; it has defeated me. But in doing so, it prepared me for everything to come. Even if I feel like I'm not ready. I suppose that by holding so tightly onto the past and wishing that nothing in my New Orleans life had changed, I have made it more difficult for me to go on with my life. And I see now that I'm going to have to change that. God knows, I wasn't ready for what Hurricane Steven did to New Orleans. But so what? No one else was, either. Now, by going back, I hope to change the memories living in my head from bitter ones to triumphant ones. Then, with God's help, I will be able to turn the page and begin a new chapter in my life.

Chapter 17 - A Nice Conversation

*D*ecember 1, 2004

*I*nhaling a dose of fresh autumn air, I exhale as I look out into the woods that are visible from Danny's guestroom balcony, which overlooks the backyard. What a relief it is to be free! Free from stress. Free from pain. Free from depression. And free from the memories that had kept me tied to one place. The place I called home—old New Orleans. The city of jazz and blues tunes, the city with a heart that never stops beating. Oh, how I love New Orleans. I don't think my love for my hometown will ever change. But I had to leave. It was entirely too much to see how the city had changed. If it hadn't been for the funeral, I wouldn't have ever gone back there.

But I had to bury my Momma. The funeral was held at Jefferson Cemetery. And as with any funeral, it was hard. Everyone showed up, even Daddy and his family. And for the first time in a long, long time, I saw Mark.

Together, we cried our hearts out, not just for Momma, but also in sheer relief. When they found

Momma's body, Mark and Daddy thought the worst had happened. They were so glad to learn I had made it out alive.

After the funeral, Daddy leisurely walked over to comfort me, and we talked briefly. He hugged me tightly and asked, "Hey, baby, how you holding up?"

Making a subtle shoulder shrug, I somberly replied, "I'm okay."

"All right. I know it's hard, going through this, but if you need to talk, I'm here."

If I need to talk. Was he serious? *After all of this time,* I thought, *he wants to be Daddy and talk all of a sudden.*

"Okay," I told him.

He planted a kiss on my cheek and began to tell me how glad he was to see that I made it out, and how hard he'd prayed and how he'd held on to the hope that me and Momma was safe. He told me how he and Mark must've searched just about every nook and cranny of New Orleans looking for me and Momma. As the months passed, he lost hope, terrified of the thought that he was going to be recovering two bodies.

With tears in his eyes and with his hands upon my shoulders, Daddy looked me square in the eyes. Then he delivered an apology, confessing that he'd done a lot of things wrong and owning up to them. I guess he'd had a lot to think about during the months he feared he'd lost us, and it made him feel a tad bit guilty. He might've said he was sorry twenty times for hurting me, Mark, and Momma. And he kept saying that he should've been there for us as we grew older. I'm sure if he could do it all over again, he would do it entirely differently. What person wouldn't?

He hugged me once more. With tears in his eyes, he looked straight into mine, as if he wanted me to feel his pain. I know the eyes are the windows to the soul, and oftentimes the truth can be seen through them, hidden beneath the web of lies.

After talking with Daddy, Mark and I had a conversation of our own. I told Mark what had happened that night, how Christy was rescued first and taken somewhere unknown, how I eventually ended up in Atlanta. He was relieved to hear that I was doing okay there.

When I asked Mark to tell his story, he said that he and Daddy went to stay with Daddy's relatives in Baton Rouge, but now Daddy was thinking about moving to Arkansas to stay. Mark might go and live with him there. Like me, he isn't sure what his future holds.

He also told me the same story Daddy told me, about how he and Daddy searched high and low for me and Momma. They looked for months and never gave up. He even told me they went to the high school and looked for me there, but I'd already left. And he and Daddy weren't sure where I'd been taken. He told me, too, that he was one of the family members who took the Kinship DNA Analysis needed to recover Momma's body from the morgue. I was wondering who it could have been.

After spending a few days with Mark, Daddy, and Daddy's family in Baton Rouge, I made arrangements with Mr. Thompson to tour New Orleans and the Lower 9th Ward. But before going back, I took some time to sit down with Daddy so I could clarify a few things about my original birth parents. Because I didn't want to bring up the subject so suddenly after the funeral, I waited for the appropriate time to talk to him. It was very apparent that he was mourning the loss of Momma much harder than I thought he would. Although he had left Momma for another woman when I was four years old, I could tell by the look on his face when I spoke with him that he wished he'd done more to make things right with her. Seeing the look of distress and deep bewilderment upon his face, I walked up to Daddy where he was sitting on the front porch of his house and smoking a cigarette.

Concerned, I leaned over to give him a hug and a kiss. He exhaled smoke from his mouth, blowing symmetrical circles, one after the other. "How's my little girl?"

Taking a seat in a nearby chair, I replied somberly, "I'm okay."

A moment of sudden quiet came, as if Daddy and I were lost for words. Not a sound could be heard for minutes, except for the chirping of a few birds in the trees around us.

Taking one last puff of his cigarette, Daddy flicked it out into the yard.

"You know, Angie, my heart is hurting right now," he said.

Looking very curiously at Daddy, I responded, "What's wrong, Daddy?"

"The pain is killing me. You know your momma was a good woman. I just wasn't a good man for her, and I knew it. I wanted to make it work, but I just couldn't. Back then, I was no good."

"Daddy, don't talk like that!" I said. "You *are* some good, and Momma knew it. If she didn't, you think she would've taken the time to be with you? You need to give yourself more credit than that."

But after I said it, feeling obligated to because I was his daughter, I pondered what I had said for a second. I thought to myself, *yeah, you really were a no-good man. You just up and left us.*

"When I first met your momma," my Daddy said, "for some reason she said she just knew I was the right man for her. But I knew I wasn't; I was a lover of many women, and settling down was hard. But she was persistent." He smiled at the memory, even while shaking his head in dismay.

All I could do was sit and listen as he poured his heart out. It was almost like I wasn't really there, as if he were talking to himself to release his pain, or searching for someone who could try to understand it.

"Your mother wanted a family so bad, and I wasn't ready, not at all." He smirked. "At least, that's what I thought. Well, she wanted to have kids, but couldn't, due to her low white blood cell count or something, so we talked about adoption."

When he said *adoption,* he caught my attention. Just the information I had hoped to hear. Sitting at the edge of my seat, I was tuned all in, waiting to hear more.

"Although I wasn't ready to have a child, let alone settle down, your momma talked me into it."

At this point I was somewhat puzzled. How the hell can someone talk you into doing something you say you don't want to do? Daddy had to come up with an excuse better than that. If he could've seen the look on my face, he'd have seen I smelled the bullshit he was telling. *If it smells like bullshit, it is bullshit.* But he wasn't really paying attention to me. He was so wrapped up in his own story, he couldn't look beyond it to see the expression on my face.

Now, it'd taken a minute for all of this to sink in because I wasn't buying it. Momma had told me part of the story already, though, so it wasn't hard to appear very interested even though I had my doubts about what he was saying. However, I reminded myself that there's two sides to every story, and this was a tale that Momma had never fully told me.

"Your momma started talking about marriage, about kids, and it scared me," my Daddy continued. "But I made a promise to her on our fourth or fifth date, back during our senior year in high school, that after college we could work on having a family of our own." He shook his head. "Never did I imagine I'd break that promise."

Daddy pulled out another cigarette and let it rest upon his lips. With the cigarette lighter in one hand, he smirked ever so slightly as he reflected on his memories.

"Angie," he whispered, "I loved your momma. But I got so caught up with other women during college, that after graduating, I felt guilty and tried to keep my promise."

He lit up the cigarette and looked at it with tears in his eyes. I could tell he'd been holding this back for some time.

"I just wish I could've told her I'm sorry for all I did to hurt her," he said.

Now the story was getting interesting, so I asked, "If you tried to keep your promise, but broke it, what happened?"

"After me and your momma got married, got the apartment, got you, I got cold feet. It was too much to bear. I wasn't ready for all of that. I thought I was, but I wasn't."

He took a puff of his lit cigarette, which had been slowly burning down while he was holding it. Then he continued.

"So, I left when you were four. Mark was getting ready to be born, and your momma was nagging me about money, bills…really, about everything imaginable."

I was trying hard not to get upset as I listened to him explain his side of the story. Part of me wanted to tell him the truth about the hurt he'd caused to Momma and to his children. But if I interrupted him now, I might never learn what had happened. So I kept my composure, although I had to work very hard to hide my anger.

Finally, I steadied myself enough to speak calmly.

"So, when you left, did you ever think about coming back?" I asked.

Daddy exhaled his last puff from his cigarette and pressed it down onto the sidearm of the chair to put it out. You could tell he did this often just by looking at the many burn marks he'd branded into the wood.

"I did," he said quietly, "but your momma wouldn't let me. After Mark was born, I wanted to come back and handle my responsibilities as a husband and dad. But your momma was so upset, she refused to let me."

I couldn't help wondering if Mark knew anything about this. As I was thinking it over, Daddy got up from his chair and leaned over the porch railing. With a bit of hesitation in his voice, he went on to tell me that Mark knew just about everything. However, he didn't know that I was adopted. He just knew that I was his sister.

"I think Momma was going to tell me before she died," I said. "I just hate that I had to find out the way I did."

"I thought you would've known by now," Daddy said.

"I wish I had. Maybe I could've found my real parents."

"It's not too late."

"So, who were they?"

Daddy turned around. He'd been gazing out over the porch railing, but now he looked me full in the face. "She was a teenage mother, someone me and your momma knew from college, and she wanted to have an abortion. Me and your momma was able to talk her into giving you up for adoption. As soon as you were born, we was at the hospital ready to get custody of you from Cheryl, who signed over her parental rights. We took you home, and it was the happiest day of our lives."

[178]

I frowned. I had a name, now, but it wasn't enough. I could feel my curiosity growing even stronger. I just *had* to learn more about Cheryl. I started wondering where she might be today. Was she still alive, and if so, where was she? Did I look anything like her, or did I look more like my biological dad? And who *was* my dad? Many questions ran through my head, but I felt a pang of sadness as I realized that my daddy almost certainly didn't have an answer.

But maybe he could tell me more. Maybe he could give me enough information to find my birth mother. So I asked Daddy if he remembered Cheryl's last name.

He thought for a minute. "I think it was Brown," he said. But he looked uncertain.

"Are you sure?" I asked.

"If I'm correct," he said, nodding. "I think that was her last name. She might be married now."

"So she would be the same age as you and Momma?" I asked.

"Yeah, about that. I think she was a year or two younger."

Now that I had her name and some idea of her age, I knew I'd be able to return home and look for her. I just wished I had the paperwork that was given to Momma and Daddy at the hospital. All of that information would have made my search a lot easier, but I knew those papers must have been destroyed in the storm, along with everything else I saw when I toured the wreckage of New Orleans and the Lower 9th Ward with Mr. Thompson.

Chapter 18 - Reality Check

*I*t was tough going back. It was hard to look at so much destruction—torn and water-damaged buildings, abandoned cars, fallen trees—and think that New Orleans could ever rebound. Traveling through the city, with Mr. Thompson as my official guide, I bore witness to incredible waste and ruin. Several times during that trip, Mr. Thompson showed me where businesses had been. According to Mr. Thompson, these and other local businesses once fueled New Orleans's economy, producing sales of over one hundred million dollars each year. The rebuilding process may take years, and it might be more than a decade before the small business owners can thrive here like they did before. For many such business owners, Steven simply put them out of business for good.

Looking at the city, I can hardly imagine how so many people survived the tragedy. So many homes were entirely destroyed, leaving behind nothing but concrete foundations filled with mud and debris. I could see how deep the water level was just by looking at the flood lines on many of the remaining buildings. Many of the historical landmarks around the tourist district near Jackson Square suffered major damage. A few of these historical landmarks dated as far back as 1862, when New Orleans was captured by Union troops that were positioned around the city.

Eventually, Mr. Thompson and I made our way into the Lower 9th Ward. Coming over the Claiborne Avenue overpass, cruel reality suddenly hit me, and I had to blink away tears. The Lower 9th Ward had been totally wiped out. There wasn't a single home or tree left standing. The only thing visible over the wreckage was the marquee for Mr. Green's Grocery, which I remember so well from when Christy and I were trapped on the roof.

The entire neighborhood looked like a landfill. I gazed around at the rubble, at the sludge left behind when the waters receded, and at the debris covering everything. Looking carefully, I was able to locate the property that Momma's house once stood on. The only thing left now was the foundation. And lying in the front yard, coated in mud, was Momma's favorite chair.

Stepping out of the city vehicle, I couldn't help but cry. I shook my head in disbelief at the senseless destruction I'd seen. Slowly, Mr. Thompson following behind, I walked over to what appeared to be the front entrance of the house and vaguely remembered that horrible Fourth of July weekend when Hurricane Steven's massive winds toppled it down.

Standing there, overawed by the destruction of my childhood home, I found it hard to move. My body shut down and went into complete shock. As I stood there, looking around, I clearly remembered what occurred the night Steven struck.

Now, I saw that Momma's house had been ripped from its foundation and pushed several feet across the street into Mr. and Mrs. Adams's front yard. Severe wind and flood damage had damaged it so badly that it was only barely standing. As for Ms. Ida Mae's house, it was blown from its foundation as well, and had rammed into the side of her next-door neighbor's house, where Mr. Stephenson lived.

There was nothing recognizable there. Nothing that was worth re-building.

Memories flashed before my eyes, memories of growing up in this neighborhood. But now I saw that the entire neighborhood was gone.

I remember Mr. Thompson consoling me with a hug as I cried.

As the tour continued, we walked for maybe twenty minutes up and down what was left of Gordon Street. That's when Mr. Thompson told me the bad news. He told me that the city was still finding bodies in swimming pools, cars and lakes. He told me that the death toll as of the time of my visit was over a thousand and still rising. He also said the bulk of the bodies were still on Interstate 10 and in the Lower 9th Ward, where only forty percent of the community was confirmed as having survived. The other sixty percent weren't as fortunate, and were either missing or known to be deceased.

When I heard that, I realized God had really been watching over Christy and me that fatal night, because we were on Interstate 10 before we ended up back home in the Lower 9th Ward. We survived both tragedies, when so many others did not.

#

Moving forward with my life, I've decided to treat each day as a new day and put the past behind me. Everything in my past is just that—the past. It is time for me to move on.

Some steps are easy. I've started to call Atlanta home since coming back from burying Momma a month ago. New Orleans is my hometown, but I no longer think of it, or talk about it, as 'home.'

Other steps are harder. Considering all the heartache and pain I've endured over the past few months, Danny and I aren't rushing into a committed relationship. He suggested we should take it one day at a time and see where things go from there, and I agreed with him. I know I still need time to heal and get myself together before I can commit to him or to any man.

There are some things I need to work on specifically, like my trust issues, and having enough faith in myself to be in a committed relationship. Believe me, I've never been in a committed relationship before, so I don't trust myself or have faith in my ability to keep and maintain one. But Danny is gradually changing that. He has embraced me with a heart full of love, something I've missed out on from my daddy, from men in general, and perhaps most, from myself.

Although Danny and I aren't really dating yet, he has vowed not to see other women, saying he's ready to settle down with just one. And he believes I'm the one woman for him. He understands my trust and faith issues, and he's okay with taking it slow. So, the thought of being in a committed relationship to Danny is not a key factor for me yet, but we're working on it. He's definitely one in a million.

When I came back from New Orleans, Danny and Brianna met me at the airport with three dozen pink roses. I will admit, it was the sweetest thing any man has done for me in a long while. I was so full of excitement to see Danny and Brianna again, I gave them the biggest hug ever. When I was gone, I did miss both of them very much. And it was written all over my face when I first saw them again. Believe me when I say I was smiling the biggest smile ever. It felt good to come back to the family I've longed for.

Danny asked how the funeral was, and I told him I was happy to have seen my uncles and aunts again. And I never knew Momma had so many friends. After several minutes of talking about lighthearted subjects, I finally broke down and told him about my biological mom, Cheryl Brown, and about how excited I was to search for her on the site findalovedone.com. Danny smiled in excitement, happy for me now that I knew more about my real momma.

And Ms. Stanley, God bless her soul, is like a second mom to me now. The day after arriving back in Atlanta, I needed a shoulder to cry on while I vented my anger over every senseless, destructive thing that had transpired in my hometown.

And like any momma, she was there to listen to my problems. She also invited Danny, Brianna and me over to the house to have dinner with them that night. She cooked lasagna, baked garlic bread, and served a nice crisp salad. Mr. Stanley served the food to us and blessed the meal. I can't help but feel that this is now my family. They've been here for me through all of my bittersweet days.

It's been a rough ride, but knowing they're here is a wonderful feeling. Nothing can compare to the love of a family.

When I look around me now, I see people who have welcomed me into their lives with open arms. People who have made me feel love like I've never felt before. The feeling is so warm, it's like I'm meant to be here.

But it can never replace the love I have inside of me for Momma, Mark, and Christy. Yes, I do miss them dearly. And there isn't a day that goes by that I'm not searching the Internet for some sign of Christy.

Long ago, Danny showed me a website that he and his remarkable staff had created, though I didn't know about that connection at the time. That site was findalovedone.com, and I posted a search notice there so that people would know that Christy and Mark were missing. I haven't received any updates about Christy, but I'm hopeful. As of today, more than twenty thousand Hurricane Steven evacuees have posted a search on findalovedone.com, and over four thousand eight hundred missing victims have been found.

When I thanked Danny for arranging the creation of that website, Danny smiled and said he doesn't want any credit for his good deeds; he just wanted to do more to help. So with the help of his staff and an extensive marketing campaign, findalovedone.com was launched in August. A thirty-second-long commercial was broadcast that month during a live television telethon which featured many famous volunteers, including some of America's top actors in movies, plays, and sitcoms, as well as musicians specializing in styles ranging from alternative rock and hip hop to rhythm and blues. The telethon was very successful, raising over eighty-five million dollars for the Hurricane Steven Relief Fund.

And according to Danny, the findalovedone.com commercial was just as successful, resulting in over four hundred thousand hits and twenty thousand postings from Hurricane Steven evacuees searching for their missing love ones.

I'm proud of Danny and his involvement with Steven. He's doing an excellent job helping to raise proceeds and awareness for missing victims. It's estimated that America has helped raise more than a billion dollars for hurricane relief and aid. That's a lot of money.

However, the cost to rebuild New Orleans is estimated at one hundred and twelve billion dollars, according to the New Orleans Redevelopment Association, a team of engineers, architects, builders, contractors, and inspectors.

Granted, America has opened its wallets in a big way to contribute to the relief efforts. But the money raised is just a bare percent of what's needed. Still, every day, the dollar amount increases. And whenever I can, I do my part to contribute as well. After visiting New Orleans, there's so much I want to do to get it beautiful and vibrant again. Every little bit helps.

Just the outpouring of donations is amazing to me. Even children are raising money, selling lemonade to help evacuees. Other businesses and organizations in Atlanta and the surrounding areas have pitched in, organizing a Day of Donation, where ten percent of their gross proceeds will go to the Hurricane Steven Relief Fund. The city of Atlanta has contributed four hundred thousand dollars to the cause, including the proceeds from the benefit concert.

Anything and everything is being done to prevent this tragedy from happening again. The Army Corps of Engineers is working to fix the levee system. Mr. Thompson says it may take six months to a year to complete the job entirely.

In order to secure the water behind the levee walls, the plan is to raise the levee system up another three feet to prevent the walls from being breached again. And in the event another possible storm occurs, be it a hurricane or a tornado, New Orleans plans to install warning systems that will sound throughout the city to prepare residents for possible evacuation.

I wish they'd taken this initiative ahead of time. But as the old saying goes, it's better late than never. I can see Steven has taught the residents of New Orleans a major lesson. I just hope they learn from it.

Chapter 19 - A Noble Cause

*D*ecember 19, 2004

*M*r. Jamal Davenport. Who would've thought I'd see his face again in close proximity? To my surprise, he's in town this weekend for a four-game series against the Atlanta Monarchs. Jamal's publicist, Andrea Houston, working with his agent, Michael Long, has scheduled a charitable auction with Jamal in each and every city the Miami Blue Fins play in as part of a campaign to raise money for the Hurricane Steven Relief Fund.

The auction is sponsored in part by the Miami Blue Fins, the Major League Baseball Association, and the opposing teams of each city, and it will be presented jointly by the Red Cross and the Give a Hand Foundation. And Armstrong Marketing is spearheading the entire campaign. So as a result, Danny and his staff received tickets to this weekend's games and the associated gala.

"Mr. Jamal Davenport," I say, grinning, while being seated before the auction. "It's nice to see you again."

He stops to give me a warm embrace as he walks past, and replies, "Angela Johnson. It's been a long time. What brings you to Atlanta?"

"Hurricane Steven," I say humorously.

Shocked and dismayed he replies, "Really, I'm so sorry to hear. How long have you been here?" he asks.

"Going on six months," I reply.

"Wow," he says, surprised. "So how are you doing? How's everybody? Are they in Atlanta with you?"

I take a deep breath and release it slowly. "I'm okay. And no one else from my family is here but me. Momma passed in the storm," I say somberly, "and I haven't seen or heard from my brother Mark since the funeral."

"I'm sorry to hear about that," Jamal says, a look of concern on his face.

"Other than that, I'm just here to try to move on with my life," I say. "So how's your mom and dad? Did they make it out safe?" I ask.

"Yeah, I got them out of town that Friday before everything happened. They didn't want to leave, but I told them they had to, and they could come back as soon as the storm was over," he says.

"Sometimes we have to do things we don't want to," I say.

"Yeah, tell me about it," he says sarcastically.

I'm not sure what he's implying, so I continue my conversation normally. "By the way, Christy and me seen you that Friday while eating lunch on the square," I say.

"Really? Why didn't you girls speak up?"

"Well, it looked like you were in a hurry, so we didn't want to bother you," I say, looking up to see Danny coming toward the table.

Looking over his shoulders, Jamal throws up his right hand and signals for the attention of a second gentlemen to make him aware of his location. "I *was* in a hurry, I was trying to get my mom and dad to the airport in time to catch their flight. I figured I'd send them to California to get away for the weekend during the storm," he says.

"That was nice of you," I say as Danny and the gentlemen, whose name, I come to learn, is Michael Risen, swiftly walk over to join us.

"Jamal, I'd like you to meet Mr. Danny Armstrong," says Michael.

"Pleasure to meet you," says Jamal.

"The pleasure is mine," Danny says as he and Jamal exchange firm handshakes.

"Danny's the owner and founder of Armstrong Marketing. His company's overseeing the marketing campaign for the city-to-city charitable auctions," Michael explains.

"I've heard a lot about you and your company. I'm glad I'm able to work with a company that prides itself on giving back to the community," says Jamal.

"Thank you. Giving back to the community has been our preferred method of operation since day one. And we're excited to be working with one of baseball's number-one players," Danny says, placing his hand onto my shoulder.

"So you know Ms. Johnson?" Jamal asks.

"Yeah, she's a good friend of mine," Danny says.

"Angela and her sister Christy and I attended college together," says Jamal.

"Really," Danny says, surprised. "Such a small world."

"Yeah, tell me about it. It's been some years, but she and Christy still look just the same," Jamal says. "Talk about coincidence. What are the chances of me seeing you and Christy within the same week? The two of you were inseparable. She has to be somewhere around here," he says, looking out over the crowd in an attempt to find her. "Were you with her earlier this week at the Detroit auction?" he asks curiously.

My eyes fill with tears and my heart races. "No, I wasn't. I haven't seen or spoken to Christy since the day she was rescued from Momma's rooftop after the hurricane." I feel shocked to realize it's been that long since I've seen my best friend. "So you seen Christy in Detroit?"

"Yeah, I seen her. She was in the audience during the auction in Detroit a few days ago," Jamal says. "But we never spoke."

"Is she okay?" I ask.

"She appeared to be okay," he says cautiously. "Is everything all right?"

With Danny's arm draped comfortably over my shoulder, I cry tears of joy. "Yeah. You're *sure* it was Christy you seen?" I say, crying.

"Yeah, I never forget a pretty face," Jamal replies.

"Are you one hundred percent sure that you seen Christy? Not someone that looks like her?" Danny questions.

Jamal nods. "I'm sure the woman I seen in Detroit was her."

That small piece of information is all I need to help me in my search. Who knows, maybe I'll be successful in finding her. I know that in a city the size of Detroit there can be more than one Christy Olsen living there, but I hope I can find the right one. I've now gotten many replies on findalovedone.com from people searching for a Christy Olsen who was last seen in New Orleans during the Fourth of July weekend, but it wasn't the Christy Olsen I'm searching for. This Christy Olsen, I was told, was from Miami. And she hasn't been seen since. I send my prayers to her family. I hope they find her soon.

Of all the places in America, I think, *Christy ended up in Detroit.* And here I am in Atlanta. Who would've thought she and I could ever be separated? Everyone who knows Christy and me also knows that we went everywhere together. We're like Thelma and Louise. She's been my best friend since grade school. I'm just glad the rescue crew took her somewhere safe. Wherever she is, I'm sure she's alive and well.

I can't bear the thought of not seeing her again. Just thinking about it, I can feel my stress level rise. But I can't let myself be a nervous wreck now; tonight is Danny's night to be in the company of his business peers and colleagues. I have to hold it together.

I focus on a more positive thought: being able to meet Christy again someday. Now that I have an idea as to where Christy is, my main concern now is locating her. It takes effort, but I refuse to let the news that Jamal just shared overwhelm me. Although my emotions are telling me that it's good to shed tears of joy and happiness at the news, it's obvious that some of that is just my trauma talking. The scars from Hurricane Steven are still here, making it harder for me to keep my composure when I feel such strong emotions. But I will not allow them to get the best of me tonight. I won't let tears ruin this moment of happiness. I'm enjoying myself tonight, and I'm surrounded by friendly people. I tell myself very firmly, *I have no reason to cry*.

That's when I realize how much I've changed. I knew in my head that my anxiety and my tendency to be overwhelmed by emotions must be getting better over time. But now I'm so much stronger than I was, and I can actually see the improvement.

I think back on the past months and realize I'm so much healthier than I was when I first came to Atlanta. Each day now I'm making progress, and bit by bit, I'm working to overcome my anxiety and depression. And I can honestly say I'm in a much better place today than I was last week or last month. There really *is* light at the end of the dark tunnel that Hurricane Steven threw me into. And every day, I can see and appreciate more of the good things in my life.

The thought of "good things" is a powerful one, and I can't help but glance over at Danny. In an instant I'm reminded of the joy he brings me each and every day that we're together. I can't help but to smile and blush in genuine happiness as he looks back at me. He makes me smile and blush all the time, it seems. I think I might be in love, genuinely in love, and it feels so good.

Looking around me, I see people swarming into the room to be seated. I suppose the auction is about to begin. Charles Ringer, the owner of the Blue Fins, and Tony Silva, the owner of the Monarchs, sit down to join Danny, Michael, Jamal, and myself at a reserved table. Mr. John Zimmerman, the director of the Red Cross, joins us as well.

In their own polite way, they greet each other. Danny introduces me as his friend to each of the men. Although I'm the only woman there, I'm honored to be in the company of such prestigious people, people who make a difference. Each of them has made a tremendous contribution to society and to America's business world.

The auction starts off with a blast. The host for the evening is none other than Danny himself, who, I might add, is doing a good job. He's not properly trained to be an auctioneer, but I'm not worried.

Celebrities of every profession, from acting, singing, and professional sports to local radio and television personalities, have been invited to attend the auction. They even bring some of their own prized possessions to auction off to in order to help hurricane victims. Jamal has given a worn autographed game jersey, which I'm sure is going to bring in a pretty penny. I'm told Jamal Davenport memorabilia is a hot commodity with baseball fans.

According to Baseball Sensation, the magazine that tracks the careers of baseball players, Jamal's rookie baseball card alone is priced at eighty-five dollars. When he graduated from South Tech, he was the number one draft pick and one of baseball's top prospects.

I never understood how anyone could spend so much money for a jersey bearing Jamal's name until now. From people who are die-hard baseball fans, to Jamal Davenport fans, to your avid sports memorabilia collectors, they are all at the auction to try to get their hands on Jamal's jersey.

I must say, Steven may have turned New Orleans upside down, but he brought together a nation and turned it right-side up. I'm just glad all the money that's being raised is really going to the recovery effort. There have been reports of some businesses accepting donations on behalf of Hurricane Steven victims that don't actually donate the money. However, I'm well aware that tonight's event is being presented by two notable charities that have a long history of reliable service. And one of them is the Give a Hand Foundation, founded in 1998 by Jamal himself, a fact which I only just became aware of as I spoke with him earlier tonight.

After an hour of non-stop entertainment, the evening comes to an end. I have to say the auction was very nice. Danny impressed me with his ability to work a crowd. And his stage presence was nice, a perfect fit for the role of a host.

I never knew so many people attended auctions before. Everyone came out tonight to help this one cause, and it wasn't about anything else. It wasn't about who had the most money or who won the most bids. It wasn't about any of that. It was about people coming together to have a good time and help with a worthy cause.

Because Danny has made reservations for a dinner at ten o'clock at a nice Italian restaurant off East Paces Ferry Road in Atlanta, he decides not to attend the after party held in the hotel's clubhouse. So after saying our farewells, we leave for the night.

I enjoy Italian food, but it's nothing like real New Orleans cooking, which I haven't had since I went back several weeks ago. Trust me—when I went back to my hometown, that's all I ate. I might've gained five pounds in that time. But I haven't had any good New Orleans cooking since I came back. And oh, how I miss the jambalaya, gumbo, red beans and rice, steamed oysters, and shrimp. Just thinking about it makes my mouth water. I'm so hungry I feel like I could eat a horse. We did eat at the auction, but it was just finger food, and that was well-digested minutes after I'd eaten it. So for right now, Italian will have to do.

I can go for some calamari or a grilled rack of lamb marinated in fresh rosemary and olive oil, or a baked fillet sautéed with seasoned vegetables and served with a slice of tiramisu. It sounds good just talking about it. As you can tell, I *have* eaten Italian before. But it's not my overall preference.

Danny and I arrive at the restaurant and are soon seated. The ambiance is so relaxing, and the décor is nice.

Not what I anticipated in a five-star restaurant, maybe, but the overall setting is good, and so far, the calamari appetizer is good. This is usually the dish I use when making my judgment of the chef's cooking.

If the appetizer isn't good, then I assure you the food isn't, either. And I've had my share of bad food at restaurants before, which isn't good because I typically wouldn't go back to patronize that restaurant again. But this restaurant is really nice. Danny tells me that because he likes the atmosphere, he comes here often to conduct business meetings.

Suddenly, a very pretty waitress who appears to be in her late twenties with the bubbliest personality walks over to take our order. Danny gets his usual—grilled fillet mignon with balsamic vinaigrette sauce. And he recommends that I try the braised veal served with roasted potatoes. It sounds promising, so I order it and give it a try.

While waiting for dinner, we engage in conversation and just enjoy each other's company.

"So are you enjoying yourself?" Danny asks.

Between the conversations from the participants and live music within the restaurant, I barely can hear him, so I lean up closer as he repeats himself louder, "Are you enjoying yourself?"

Smiling bashfully I reply, "Yeah, I needed this."

"That's good. I wanted to treat you to a special evening to take your mind off some of the things going on in your world," he says. "I know the past few months have been hard on you, so I wanted to get you out so you could have a good time."

"I really appreciate it, and you're right—I did need this."

"You and I both. I haven't gotten the opportunity to get out in a while either—so I thought, who would be the most appropriate person to spend the evening with, besides you?" he says, and he takes a sip of water. After working sixty-plus hours a week, I'm not surprised he needed this time as much as I did. I'm glad his mother kept Brianna this weekend. She insists that he ought to get out more.

After waiting patiently for our drinks and food to arrive, our waitress finally appears, "Hello, I'm back. I'm so sorry for the delay. It's a busy night tonight," she says delightfully. "I have a braised veal served with roasted potatoes, and a nice glass of Pink Moscato for the lady," she slowly removes items from her tray and places everything in front of me. "And for the fine gentlemen, we have a grilled fillet mignon with balsamic vinaigrette sauce, and a very nice glass of Amalaya Malbec."

"Thank you," Danny says.

"Is there anything else I can get for you?" she asks.

"No thank you, everything is fine," says Danny.

"Okay, well if you're interested in dessert, we have a great selection on the menu to choose from," she says excitedly.

"All right, thank you. We'll be sure to take a look at it when we're done," Danny says.

"Okay, I'll be back to check on you to see if you would like any, or just need anything else. In the meantime enjoy your meal," she says kindly.

"Will do, and thank you very much," Danny says smiling.

Such a gentlemen he is.

"I've been thinking," Danny says while placing his wine onto the table.

"About?"

"How about after all of this is said and done, we take a nice get-away vacation and ease our minds? I would love for us to spend a week in the Caribbean. Just let me know where you want to go and when."

I can't help but to blush. I've never before felt love so genuine from a man. It almost feels too good to be true. Besides, I've never been to the Caribbean, it would be a nice get away.

Taking my napkin from where it is resting on my lap, I wipe my mouth before responding. "So, wherever I'd like to go and when?"

"You name the place and the time, and we're off."

I wonder whether he can see how happy I am by the dim light of the dining room. I feel so happy, I almost feel like I'm glowing.

I ask, "That simple?"

"That simple."

"Can we go to Dubai?" I ask.

Danny laughs slightly as he takes another sip of his sweet tea. "Dubai? Although Dubai isn't in the Caribbean, we can go there. We can go wherever. I just figured on the Caribbean because the weather is really nice there. But we could also try someplace like Dubai, or maybe check out Bora Bora, if you're interested in visiting French Polynesia."

"Bora Bora," I say. I would never have dreamed I'd get to visit such a place, especially not with someone as special as Danny, but the opportunity is right here in front of me.

"Bora Bora, Jamaica, the Bahamas, Aruba…you name it, we'll go. But if you really want to go to Dubai, we can do that, too. We just have to get you a passport so we can travel."

Part of me thinks I should've named Hawaii or some country in Europe, but the rest of me is still fairly stunned. I look at Danny as if to say, *really, we can just go to Dubai?* Not that I even know where the hell Dubai is, honestly, or how to get there; it just popped into my head. Almost a year ago, now, I overheard Mr. Thompson mention he was taking his wife there for their twenty-fifth wedding anniversary. I saw some pictures of the place when Mr. Thompson told me to go to a website advertising vacation packages to get some flight and hotel information for him. And I must say that from what I've seen, Dubai is truly beautiful.

Looking into Danny's beautiful brown eyes, I say, truthfully, "I'd love to go anywhere, as long as we're together."

Our conversation is briefly interrupted as the waitress returns, "Hello, hope you all are enjoying your meal. Is everything okay, do you need anything?"

"No thanks, everything is just fine."

"Ok, and would you like another glass of wine," she asks Danny.

"No thank you, I'm okay."

"And you ma'am, would you like some more Moscato?"

"No thank you, I'm okay as well," I reply.

"Great. Well would you be trying some of our nice deserts tonight?" the waitress kindly asks.

Danny looks at me for an answer. I'm not sure what he'd like me to say, but I reply nicely, as I blush, "No thank you, I'm quite stuffed right now."

"And you sir, any desert?"

"No ma'am, I'm okay," Danny says.

"Well, if that would be all, I shall return with your bill," she says.

"Thank you," Danny replies.

Smiling like a kid at Christmas time, I grab Danny's well-manicured hands and hold them gently. I can't help but tell him how much I appreciate him. I gather my nerves to tell him that I've fallen in love with him and that I'm looking forward to spending the rest of my life with him and Brianna. But it's not easy to say those all-important words.

Trying to compose myself, I start blushing. I feel embarrassed about blushing so easily, so I try not to draw attention to the motion as I place my hands over part of my face to cover my shyness.

Danny looks at me, and it doesn't make my blushing any better. "Are you blushing? Are you turning red on me?" he asks. He gives me a vibrant smile.

Taking a small peek through my hands—as if such a small gesture could keep Danny from noticing—I blush like never before. Danny reaches over and carefully removes my hands from my face. He looks at me, and I can tell that he knows I'm embarrassed, but even though I feel bad about how visibly I reacted, he just smiles at me and accepts it. Then he lifts one of my hands, and slowly but gently kisses my right hand.

With a huge smile on his face, he looks at me, still holding my hand, and says, "I'm in love with you, too. Never did I think I'd find you—someone who I could love without any regrets. It's funny, but I never believed in love at first sight until you came along."

His smile fades, and his tone grows solemn. "It's been only few months since we've met," he says, "and I've invited you into my world and crowned you my Queen. Ms. Angela Johnson," he adds, looking me soberly in the eyes, "I'm ready to be one hundred percent committed to you, if you'll allow me."

For a moment, I'm shocked beyond belief. I sit in awed silence for a moment, trying to make sense of what I've just heard. It seems almost unreal.

Staring at Danny, I can still see his mouth moving, but my mind is racing. It's as though everything around me has gone completely silent in the wake of what he just said to me. But the rest of the world doesn't matter. It's just me and Danny, and for a moment, the world around us seems almost obsolete.

But then I come back to myself in a rush. Danny is still looking at me, waiting for an answer.

I swallow and smile at him.

"Baby," I say, speaking slowly to keep my voice from wobbling, "I'm willing to go with you wherever. I've never met a man who genuinely loves me. And I'd hate to let go of it, or of you."

I take a deep breath. "Danny, I want to be totally committed to you, too."

And then my voice fails me, but I don't need it, and Danny doesn't need to say anything else, either. Looking into each other's eyes, we hold hands and smile. Together.

Although this evening with Danny is nice, my mind keeps returning to Christy. Danny knows I'm worried, because I keep talking about her. But he's so understanding that he's not allowing it to interfere with our night. So he talks to me to help keep me motivated. He even insists that we leave early so we can get home to search for her. He can tell my mind has been racing ever since Jamal said he had seen Christy in Detroit. I just hope she's still there.

Chapter 20 - No News like Good News

*J*anuary 27, 2005

*T*he search for Christy is over. News has circulated over findalovedone.com that Christy Olsen's body has been found today, floating facedown in a retention pond. Friends I've become associated with from findalovedone.com send me their condolences, along with dozens of emails notifying me of the discovered remains. It looks as though she was murdered. And the body could've been left there for more than a month.

The news hits me so hard, I don't have time to think straight. I can only cry as I read more. Could this be true? Not again, I pray silently. I can't take this. So I log off the computer, bury my head in my hands, and cry.

Without even thinking about it, I call Danny to tell him the news.

He sounds so happy to hear from me as he asks, "Hey baby, what's going on?"

In moments, I've broken down crying. "Christy's dead," I say.

"What?" he asks, surprised and concerned. "When did you find this out?"

"Just now," I tell him. "Several people I've met on findalovedone.com sent me emails notifying me of her murder."

Taking a deep breath to give him time to reflect, Danny gently asks, "What happened? When did they find her body?"

It is ever so hard to fight back my tears as I reply, "Today. They found her today. The news article said she was raped and strangled."

Concerned, he asks, "Where did this happen?"

"They found her facedown in a retention pond," I say, crying.

Danny takes a deep breath and replies, "I'm coming home. I'll be there in a minute." Just like that, like a perfect gentleman, he hangs up the phone to rush to my side.

I force myself to calm down, gather my thoughts, and relax. If my memory serves me well, I can clearly remember the Christy Olsen who was last seen in New Orleans during the Fourth of July hurricane. I recall Jamal telling me that he'd seen Christy in Detroit, but anything can happen overnight. Oh God, what am I saying? My mind is racing faster than I can react. *Get a grip, Angela,* I tell myself fiercely, *and think!*

Wiping the tears away from my eyes, I determinedly log back onto the computer in order to verify the news of Christy's murder for myself. After several minutes of browsing, I come across several articles associated with the murder of Christy Olsen. Reading the horrific news of her death, I become an emotional wreck as my heart pounds in my chest. Reading Christy Olsen's description, I'm suddenly torn between terrible sadness and incredible elation. Judging by the pictures in the news articles, she was a beautiful black woman, five feet six inches tall, who was in her mid-twenties. But it's not my Christy. Even without a picture, the height difference alone would have told me. I don't know whether to celebrate that it's not my sister Christy, or if I should feel sad for the mother that lost a beautiful daughter to a horrific crime.

Taking a moment of silence for the Christy Olsen I never knew, I get up from Danny's computer and kneel on the ground to pray.

"Heavenly Father who watches over me in my time of need, I thank you for keeping me safe throughout the past six months, and pray that you continue to keep me, Mark, and Christy safe within your arms. And Father God, we send our love and prayers on behalf of Mr. and Mrs. Olsen. We pray that you keep them strong in this difficult time. Amen."

Rising from my prayer, I sit at the head of Danny's bed, pick up the phone and attempt to call him at his office before he leaves, but to no avail—his secretary says he's already gone home for the day. So I call his mobile phone.

"Hey baby," I say, smiling with joy.

"Hey," he replies. "I'm on my way. I'm about to get into the car right now. You're okay?" Danny asks.

"Yeah, I'm okay," I say. "You don't have to come home. I'm fine."

"Are you sure? Because I can still come home if you need me to."

"Thanks, but I'm okay. I kind of jumped the gun. The news is about the Christy Olsen from Miami. She was last seen in New Orleans during the Fourth of July Music Festival," I say, breathing a huge sigh of relief.

"So it's not your sister? Not the Christy Olsen you know?" Danny asks.

"No, it isn't. Thank God," I say. Words have never been so heartfelt. "I'm okay, baby. I'm just going to sit here, gather myself together, and get back online to reach out to everyone who took the time to let me know." An idea springs up. "And I should try to reach her parents and send my condolences. They should know about this, if they haven't found out already."

"Okay, that sounds good. Maybe we can send them some flowers or something," he says.

"That would be nice. I'll see you when you get home. I love you," I say.

"I love you, too," he replies, and ends the call.

For a moment, I sit there, stunned in the best way possible.

I love you, I'd said. What the hell am I saying? Where did *that* come from? But he said it too! Am I really falling in love? Is this what falling in love means?

I shake my head and go to the computer. I'm sure I'll figure it out soon. But right now, I need to let Christy-Olsen-from-Miami's parents know about what happened to their daughter.

After another half an hour of searching the Internet, I locate Mr. and Mrs. Olsen and email them my condolences. I've just sent the message when I hear the door open and Danny arrives home anyway.

He says he's just stopping by to get something to eat since he was already on his way. But I really think he's just worried about me. Walking in the house, he kisses me on the cheek and wraps his arms around me for a moment to comfort me before he goes into the kitchen.

Only a few minutes later, just as I'm logging off the computer for the day, Ms. Stanley calls. When I told her about where Christy had ended up, she told me she would talk to some friends of hers at the Red Cross and see what she could find out. That was nearly a month ago. But now, Mrs. Stanley has great news. She has found the phone number for the Red Cross center in Detroit. According to her, if Christy's in Detroit, nine times out of ten she should be listed in the Red Cross database. It sounds as though everyone that went to the Red Cross for assistance had to fill out the same information to enter a housing center that I had to fill out. I know from experience that the information form just required a name, last known address, and social security number, but at least it's a place to start.

Ms. Stanley and I converse a little before I say goodbye. As always, she wishes me luck with reaching Christy.

At first, I am too afraid of hearing that Christy isn't listed in the Red Cross database to call. But I tell myself that if I don't, I may never find her. So, with butterflies in my stomach, I finally I get up the nerve to pick up the phone. Then I dial the number, but I hang up as soon as it starts to ring. When I put the phone down, my hands are shaking.

Staring at the number, I wonder whether I should call again. I'm incredibly nervous. I don't know what they're going to tell me. But I'll never know if I don't call. Trying to settle my nerves and ease away my fears, I take a deep breath and exhale. Then I take another breath.

After the fifth or sixth breath, I finally get up the nerve to call. When the receptionist answers, I don't hang up the phone. Instead, I speak with him and get my questions about Christy's whereabouts answered in a prompt and professional manner. I'm glad he was so kind— I think if he'd even done so much as coughed when I didn't expect it, I might have dropped the phone from nervousness.

But with his assistance, I am given a phone number where I can contact Christy at a hotel the Red Cross and FEMA placed her in, along with several dozen other hurricane victims. Sighing my relief, I politely thank him for his help and I hang up the phone so I can call Christy's number.

Before I can even lift the phone again, the phone rings.

"Hello," I say, pressing it to my ear.

"May I speak with Ms. Angela Johnson?" the masculine voice asks.

"This is she," I say, wondering who this might be.

"This is Mr. Vincent Bedford. I'm calling from Trinity Corp. in Atlanta. How are you doing?"

I'm a bit surprised to hear from Trinity after so long, but I reply, "Okay so far."

"That's good. I know it's been a while since our initial interview. But I was calling to see if you're still interested in working for Trinity Corp."

Filled with excitement, I quickly reply, "Sure, I would love to."

"Great. Are you still willing to relocate?" Mr. Bedford asks.

Boy, was I ever unprepared for this day. I've talked about working for Trinity, but as the weeks passed without a word, I stopped expecting the day would come when I would be offered a job, let alone a job in a location other than Atlanta.

Very hesitantly, I ask, "And where is this job located?"

"San Francisco," Mr. Bedford says. "The position is for an Executive Assistant. It comes with a nice salary and excellent benefits."

"When is the starting date?" I ask.

"The position needs to be filled immediately. So, if you accept the job, the Office Manager will be expecting you in the office first thing on Monday," he says. "I know it's very short notice, but I believe you are the perfect candidate for this position."

Stalling, I ask, "Mind if I get back to you with an answer later today?"

"Sure, I understand you need time to think it over," Mr. Bedford says. "But make sure you call me back with an answer today, because I need to notify the Office Manager in San Francisco of your decision."

"Okay," I say excitedly.

With my stress level mounting, something of my concern must have shown on my face, because Danny places his manly hands on my shoulders and gently begins to massage the tension away. I close my eyes and relax, leaning into him. My mind drifts away into paradise, escaping the heartfelt pain of my past and every thought or worry that has ever entered my mind.

Suddenly, I lose track of what I'm thinking. And very seductively, I start to moan. *My God, what is this man doing to me?* I ask myself.

With every stroke of his hands, my mind wanders into uncharted sexual grounds beyond anything I've ever dreamed of. I feel like I can't take this anymore. Thoughts and fantasies of making love to Danny overcome my normal reluctance as my heart and my body language scream, *Take me!*

Instantly, I'm swept away, falling into bliss, and the moment becomes intensely heated with the passion of every kiss he is sharing with me. I can't believe I'm about to make love to Danny. I've known him for only a few months. Has he been tested for HIV? The ninety-day rule has expired, but am I really ready for this sexual experience?

The thought of having sex with him races through my head, as my body and heart say *yes* and my mind says *no.* As parts of my caramel-hued body are slowly exposed, Danny caresses the upper parts of my nude frame, his hands stroking every portion of my breasts, the curves of my hips, touching my thighs so delicately that it's almost hypnotizing. I squirm as chills run through me, taking over my body. From every kiss of his lips gently caressing my body like a subtle brush stroke on a canvas, to every firm touch of his hands moving majestically up and down and all over, touching places that haven't been touched in years, I'm utterly taken in by the foreplay. And very carefully, very affectionately, he enters me, sending my hormones racing to their peak.

Suddenly, I'm completely wrapped up in the moment, as every part of me trembles at his slightest touch. Gently he makes love to me, studying my body language carefully and passionately before every move, making a connection that lets the two of us perform like synchronized ballerinas dancing. And all the while, his eyes are fixated on mine, telling me how good it feels as he looks deep into my brown eyes. I'm completely mesmerized just looking at him.

I'm totally as one with him as he moves left and right, up and down, back and forth. With my mind in total bliss, I'm tossed and flipped with such passion in every sexual position imaginable, and before I know it, I've had multiple orgasms.

Damn, what just happened? part of me asks.

And my heart answers. *This man has just made love to me as if I'm the only woman he's ever yearned for.* I didn't expect all this, but it's a good thing

But I continue to fret. *Is this how he makes love to everyone, or is it just me?*

After an hour of heavy lovemaking, I sit in silence with a guilty conscience as I question my morals. Here I am, lying in bed with a man I've known for only a few months, and I just made love to him without any protection.

What was I thinking? A better question: was I thinking at all? Or was my body in control of the entire experience? I think my body took over.

I soon begin to question myself even more. *God,* I think, *I hope Danny doesn't have any sexually transmitted diseases, let alone HIV.* That would be devastating. Can I live with the thought of knowing he has HIV? Could I continue to be in a sexually committed relationship with him? Not only that—what if he'd gotten me pregnant? Am I really ready for a baby?

But this isn't helping. I have many questions, and I know exactly who to talk to in order to get the answers I need.

Looking over at Danny as he lies asleep next to me, I wake him with a gentle pat on the back. He rolls onto his side and responds, smiling gently, "Yeah, baby?"

Without any hesitation, I ask, "Have you been tested?"

Smiling even wider, he says, "Yeah, three months ago, and I'm negative. Don't worry, I've been abstinent for a year, but I get tested regularly just to be on the safe side. So, what about you? Have you been tested?" he asks.

"Yes," I say. "Two months ago. I'm also negative."

With that out of the way, I ask why we didn't use any protection, and learn that his answer was as simple as my own.

"I got caught up in the heat of the moment," he says. "I know it's not a logical explanation, but the foreplay was intense."

Now *that* I can agree on, but still, what the hell were we thinking? I don't doubt his answers, but I'd rather be safe than sorry, so I quietly ask him, "Can we take a test together tomorrow?"

With no hesitation, he replies, "Sure."

[209]

And I reach out, hugging him fiercely. He wasn't expecting this, but he embraces me anyway. We hold each other for a while, just breathing. Together.

#

Sometime afterward, Danny and I talk about taking the relationship to the next step as we continue to lie together, entwined in each other's arms. I tell him I don't make love to just any man without protection unless we have an emotional bond. And I feel that over the past few months, Danny and I have established that bond.

I'd like for the relationship to be closer than what it currently is, and I tell him so. Hearing my words, Danny smiles his agreement and seals it with a kiss. I feel a thrill go down my spine. I suppose we just became more than just friends. *Now,* I think, nestling my body against his, *all I have to do is talk to him about that job offer.*

Chapter 21 - Happy New Year

*J*anuary 28, 2004

*W*hen I wake up this morning, I'm greeted with the glorious aroma of freshly-brewed coffee, sizzling bacon, and blueberry pancakes wafting from Danny's kitchen. Tucked away nice and warm in Danny's king-sized bed with nothing but a double extra-large T-shirt on my nude body, I get up, pull on a pair of pants, and follow the scent downstairs.

Walking toward the kitchen, I notice Danny sitting at the dining room table. *It's nine thirty in the morning,* I think happily, *and I'm awakening to breakfast, a wonderful man and a beautiful child.* It's so surreal to think that it's as if I were waking up to my own husband and daughter. In just a matter of months, I have found a wonderful, loving family.

Gradually, I make my way over to the table. Danny says good morning as he feeds Brianna sliced pancakes and she sits in her highchair, smiling at the world.

Suddenly, Danny stands up straight, then sweeps me off my feet with a huge hug and a kiss that's so welcoming it's like I can feel the happiness inside of him the way your skin feels the warm rays from the sun. It's almost like his heart has wanted me near him all along. And ever since we made love yesterday, I've yearned for his affection so strongly that I can tell my heart wanted to be near Danny, too. I don't know exactly what's going on, but I can tell I'm falling in love with him because the emotions I feel for Danny are only getting stronger and stronger.

I don't know what it was he did to me last night, but making love to Danny was by far the best sexual experience I've had since losing my virginity at twenty years old. Although it was somewhat painful, my first sexual experience made me feel that having sex with a man was the most pleasurable feeling I could ever have. But making love to Danny last night sent chills all through my body. I was so excited I could barely control myself. It felt good to make love to the one man I'd like to spend the rest of my life with.

Since coming to Atlanta, this old heart of mine has been though a lot of hurt. Constantly thinking about Momma, Mark, and Christy had me so worried that it took a toll on me mentally, physically, emotionally, and spiritually. I began to feel as though my heart had been shattered into a thousand pieces, and couldn't nothing or nobody mend my broken heart. But now that I have learned to deal with the heartache and pain caused by Hurricane Steven, I can finally open up my heart and let love in once again.

So here I am, standing in the arms of the man I've been praying to God for all of my life. I can feel his chest bulging underneath his white-collared button-down shirt, and when Danny wraps his manly hands around my tiny waist and pulls me closer, I feel every part of my body get weak, as if it would quiver from the slightest touch. Gazing into his brown eyes, the moment overcomes me, and I whisper the three words I vowed never to say unless I meant them totally, without reservation: "I love you." Once again, the words flow easily from my mouth, propelled by feelings so strong that I have no recourse but to tell him how much I care.

And with a sensual kiss on my lips, Danny tells me that he loves me, too. It's the most wonderful feeling I've had since finding out Christy is still alive. Breaking away from our little escapade, Danny walks over to the kitchen island to fix me a cup of coffee and a plate of breakfast while I take a seat at the dining table. Leaning over the table, I give Brianna a morning kiss on her cheek as she smiles ever so brightly. She is so precious to me. I just want to be a good mother to her. I love her so, so much.

Danny walks over and places the coffee and breakfast plate on the table for me.

"So, what are your plans for today?" he asks, and kisses me on my forehead.

Taking a sip of coffee, I blush, then reply, "I was going to try and call Christy a little later on. You want me to watch Brianna?"

Approaching Brianna from the other side, Danny thinks a moment before answering. "No," he decides. "You have things to do. I wouldn't want her to be in your way. I'll take her to the daycare," he says, removing her from the highchair.

"I don't have much to do," I say. "It won't be a problem, I can watch her. Besides, I was just going to call Christy."

"And how were you able to get a number to where she's at?" he asks, puzzled, while holding Brianna in his arms.

"Ms. Stanley," I say.

"That was nice of her. How's she doing?" he asks, while placing Brianna on the floor. "She's doing well?"

I reply as I take a small portion of bacon to eat.

"That's great! Next time you speak with her, tell her I said hi," he says, while putting on his royal blue blazer jacket that complements his royal blue suit.

"I will," I say. Adjusting his royal blue and orange-striped tie, Danny gathers up his briefcase, leans down to kiss Brianna and me goodbye, and walks into the garage adjacent to the kitchen. I call out to Danny that I love him, and he replies that he loves me, too.

With a huge smile on my face, I take one more sip of coffee before getting up from the table to dispose of my unfinished breakfast, which is now too cold to eat. Placing my dishes in the dishwasher, I start to think about my plans for the future and how they will affect my relationship with Danny and Brianna.

After talking to Mr. Bedford yesterday with regard to the job offer at Trinity's San Francisco branch, I'm left to wonder what impact my decision will have, now that Danny and I have taken our relationship to another level, and what I will have to sacrifice to make it work.

#

Almost two hours later, I'm helping Brianna move around the house. Brianna is still learning how to walk, so she holds onto my left leg for leverage as I walk slowly with her across the room. When she staggers and stumbles off balance, I reach down to pick her up so she won't fall. With pigtails and pink bows in her hair, she yawns and rubs her eyes. I can tell she's getting sleepy. It's eleven-thirty in the morning and she's been up for a few hours now. But I won't put her to sleep just yet. I'll try to keep her up until twelve if I can, so she can get a nice nap at noon. Until then, I guess she'll just have to be a little irritable.

Noticing Brianna's eyelids getting droopier, I put her down again so that we can walk around the house. Maybe the activity will keep her awake. Carefully, we walk into the family room to turn on the television, then proceed upstairs into the guestroom, with me helping her up every step. Fighting to stay awake, Brianna eyes become heavier and her little head sways back and forth. I can tell she's getting sleepier, but it's not naptime yet.

Taking her by the hand, Brianna and I slowly walk back downstairs into the family room. With her pacifier in her mouth, I sit her on the floor in front of her toys, and she starts contentedly playing with them as I sit on the couch to call Christy.

Picking up the phone, I dial the number for the hotel. It rings twice, then I hear Christy's voice for the first time since she disappeared into the helicopter and vanished from sight.

"Hello?" she says.

"Christy?" I ask. I can tell I'm about to cry, but for once, the tears are tears of pure joy. "Christy, is that you?"

"Yes," she says hesitantly, uncertain as to who's asking. "Who is this?"

"Oh my God, oh my God," I say, crying now. "It's you! I can't believe this, it's really you!"

Christy suddenly shrieks.

"Angela, is that *you*? I can't believe this!"

"Yes," I say, trying to fight back my tears.

"Oh my God, this can't be real. Are you serious?" she says, crying. "Angela, I hadn't heard anything for so long. Is this really you?"

"Yes, it's me," I say.

Christy exclaims, "You don't know how happy I am to hear your voice. I thought you were dead!" She's crying just as hard as I am.

"Why did you think that?" I say, alarmed. "Wasn't I alive when you last seen me?"

"Yeah, but then I heard that the helicopters were running out of gas and couldn't make any more trips that day. And we were so weak, I didn't think you could last but a few hours. I never thought I'd hear from you again," she says, sobbing as she speaks.

"And you figured I was dead?" I ask.

"I don't know what I was thinking, to tell you the truth," she says. "So much had gone wrong, and I had such a fever I couldn't think straight." I hear her swallow a lump in her throat. "Ever since that day I was rescued, I've been so traumatized by the memories. Everything I remember from those days used to send me into a panic. My mind played so many tricks on me, that I started to wonder, was it you or Momma's body floating in the water? Or was it some stranger, and my mind was playing another trick?" She takes a deep breath to calm herself. "That thought haunted me so much."

"It was Momma, Christy," I tell her, crying. "It was Momma."

"Oh, God," Christy sobs. "I had a feeling, I just didn't want to believe it."

"It's okay, baby," I tell her. "I'm sorry, but it's true." I try to think of some better subject. "So how's your leg?" I ask.

"Oh, it couldn't be better," she says, sounding relieved. "I just had my cast removed two weeks ago. My leg was broken in two places. I was rushed straight to the hospital as soon as they landed, and then I was bedridden for maybe a month. After that, the Red Cross and FEMA put me up in a hotel," she says. "So have you been back home?"

"I went back to New Orleans a month ago to bury Momma at Jefferson Cemetery," I say. I stop talking for a moment while Christy and I shed tears together.

"I hate that I wasn't there," she says.

"It's okay," I say. "You know Momma would understand."

With so much on our minds, Christy and I continue our discussion for hours about our ordeal after Hurricane Steven, only pausing long enough for me to take care of Brianna. Mostly, she plays with her toys, walks around by using the couch to lean on for balance, or rests contentedly with one hand brushing against my legs.

I tell Christy that a rescue team did come back to get me, two days after Christy'd been picked up from Momma's rooftop. She can hardly believe I was left there that long. I told her that all the while I was waiting, I couldn't help but to stare at Momma's then-bloated body as it floated a short distance from where I sat on the roof. During this time, I vaguely remember that I became delusional due to heat exhaustion and the lack of food and good water. And when I fell asleep, I was woken by a crewmember from a rescue team screaming in my ear.

In turn, Christy tells me that after she was rescued, she and fifteen other Hurricane Steven victims were taken to Dearborn Air Force Base and then flown directly to Detroit, where they arrived the same day.

Because she hates being alone in a city with a bunch of strangers, Christy tells me she rarely gets out of the hotel for fresh air. So she stays inside a majority of the time, thinking about what happened and crying about her family and friends, hoping they're all still alive. With depression and stress taking their toll, she says it's painful being without us.

Trust me, I understand her pain. And now that she's got solid reassurance that I'm alive, I will try to make plans to visit her soon to help ease some of the pain.

I tell Christy to hold on so I can take a moment's break from the conversation and lay Brianna down to sleep. Feeling like Brianna's my own child, I pick her up off the floor where she had lain on her side near my feet, sleeping like a baby. She looks so adorable. With a huge smile on my face, I kiss her on the cheek and lay her down on the opposite end of the couch. With Brianna now asleep, I'm able to take a nice shower and get myself ready for the day, so I tell Christy I'll call her back later on to discuss arrangements for me to come visit her in Detroit.

Chapter 22 - Here We Go

*J*anuary 30, 2005

"*I* love you," are the last three words I hear from Danny when he drops me off at Atlanta International Airport for my Sunday morning flight. It's hard leaving him and Brianna behind. I knew the day was bound to come, but I never thought I'd be taking it so hard. I find it incredibly difficult to leave the man I've come to love. But I know I'll see him and Brianna again. No matter what else may happen, I know I'll come back to Atlanta.

With tears in my eyes, I board the airplane and prepare myself for a long flight. As I relax into my seat, my mind drifts, and I start to reminisce.

Although New Orleans is now a thing of the past, I can't help but to think now and again about the place I once called home. I'm worried about the future of the city. When will it be rebuilt, and at what cost? The city doesn't have enough capital in reserve to support the city payroll or to start to rebuild.

Without revenue coming in from tourists and local commerce, rebuilding the city may take years unless developers express a keen interest in buying land to redevelop on. The question, then, is whether anyone will return once developers rebuild, if the cost of living becomes more expensive. The latest news updates say that the city of New Orleans may be filing for bankruptcy sometime in the upcoming week. So, it's obvious that the city's in financial ruin. Even with federal aid, the city is struggling to pay the bills.

Steven has affected everyone financially, including me. Due to insurance claim delays and the recent actions of the New Orleans Redevelopment Association, the rebuilding process has been difficult. With a majority of the worst damage in the Lower 9th Ward, Mr. Thompson's emailed updates tell me that a great deal of the time and manpower needed to clean up the city is going to be focused on the Lower 9th Ward.

It's been a long time since I've seen Christy, and I can't wait to see her again. I can clearly remember the last time I saw her, and it kills me inside every time I think of that night. But I've learned to handle those memories and even thrive in spite of them. So here I am—taking my life in a new direction.

Christy and I have been through a lot together. Speaking with her yesterday brought back so many memories. We talked, of all things, about prom night in our junior year of high school. Our dates, who were also best friends, had made plans for everyone to eat dinner at some fancy restaurant before attending the prom. The restaurant was nice, but none of the four of us had a clue about fondue, let alone how to prepare it the right way. So we sort of experimented with the appetizer, but we didn't get to eat much of it.

Once the meal arrived, we all sat there staring at it, wondering why it wasn't cooked. Then we came to find out we had to cook it ourselves. We had ordered alligator, because it was expensive and we were curious about trying it, but none of us had had any idea about what we were getting. The alligator was well-seasoned, and it didn't taste anything like what I expected, but it tasted okay.

When I spoke to Christy on Friday, I admitted for the first time ever that I didn't think the alligator was worth the money. She broke up laughing and told me that she'd thought the same thing, and we both cracked up. Our poor dates! Christy and I had eaten the meal and pretended like it was the best thing ever just so they wouldn't feel bad.

In the end, our dates had just wanted to make the night special, so they thought it was worth every penny. They paid for the meal and were happy. However, Christy and I both thought it was crazy to pay that kind of money for something you had to prepare yourself.

It was good to hear Christy laugh so hard. So we kept talking, remembering good times. I reminded her that on that prom night, Christy and I looked like beautiful princesses, and the pictures we had taken for us were really nice. Christy agrees that it was fun, but pointed out that those pictures were probably all washed away during Hurricane Steven. I agreed with her, but said that as long as I have them in my heart, I can never forget those good times.

By the time Christy and I said farewell for the night, I think she was feeling a lot better. And that's what matters. Not pictures or favorite chairs or even the houses we grew up in. As long as the people who matter are safe, healthy, and happy, anything else is extra.

#

The weekend of July 4th, 2004 is a time I'll never forget. Hurricane Steven's arrival permanently altered my plans for raising a family in New Orleans. Never had I imagined the effects that a single day could have on my life. I had always dreamed of raising a family in New Orleans, of trying to keep the family roots there, but that dream has disappeared.

Like many evacuees, I had high hopes of returning, only to find that there wasn't anything in New Orleans to return to. My plans were finally and thoroughly shattered when I went back for Momma's funeral. The devastation was unbearable, and I decided not to return. Instead, I've found love in Danny Armstrong, the most wonderful man God could've ever created to grace my presence.

Just saying his name makes me blush. I haven't been gone an hour yet and I miss him and Brianna already. I can only imagine how homesick I'll be in the next couple of days. But I think I'll manage to be okay until I return to Atlanta. I believe I can make it until then. If not, that's fine, too. I'll just be back sooner than I'd expected.

Atlanta has treated me well. The southern hospitality there is so warm and inviting. I know now why so many people are choosing to move there. People from all around the world are making Atlanta their home. And the city is growing every day. No wonder so many Hurricane Steven evacuees have decided to make the city their new home.

I'll be back, I know. Atlanta's a city you can't help but to love. Its overall atmosphere is perfect, and it is so safe that at any time during the year you can enjoy a nice night out on the town without the hassle of being mugged. It appears that the city even keeps criminal activities under control.

Of course, every city has its share of crime, though I never heard much about Atlanta's criminal activity the way I heard about crime when I lived in New Orleans. I just hope that where I'm going the crime rate isn't so bad.

Hours later, the pilot announces our arrival at San Francisco International Airport. I can hardly believe it. Here I am in San Francisco, California for the first time. I've come a long way since leaving New Orleans. And I can't wait to call Danny and Christy to let them know I've arrived.

- *END* –

His Story: Coming Soon

A Thousand Miles Away

It's been well over a week since I've been back home. The visit to San Francisco was well worth it. I haven't seen Angela since she left Atlanta a month ago to work for one of America's prestigious hotel chains, Trinity Corp. Displaced from New Orleans after the tragedies of Hurricane Steven, she and I first met at a local park in the city of Atlanta on a warm Spring day at a vending cart. I remember that day very well, I had a rough day at work and to ease my mind, I decided to take a walk through the park with the only girl in my life. It was from that day on, seven months ago, that Angela became my best friend, my partner, and my lover. She has balanced my life as a single parent and successful entrepreneur, that I'm proud to have met her. During the five months that she was in Atlanta, she made such a difference in my life, helping me to become a better man than the man I used to be—a man who played on the hearts of many women with little concern.

Chapter One—Who Is It?

Suddenly, there's a knock on my door. "Come in." The door swings gently open, and from the corner of my eye, I look up to see this lovely silhouette of a woman.

"Hey baby," I say in surprise, smiling from ear to ear as I rise from my desk to greet her, "So what brings you here?" Entering into my office she walks in with a mission. Seductively canvassing the room for any potential witnesses that could look inside, she leans toward me in the most intimate way as she loosens my tie and walks me back into my chair, where I fall. Caught entirely off-guard by her actions, I'm at a loss for words to say stop. Passionately, we kiss as she straddles her body upon my lap. *What am I doing?* My mind races uncontrollably for an answer, but there isn't one. I'm enjoying the moment too much. Here I am in my office, and I'm about to take her. Thrusting her sexy frame upon my desk, I lay her out and gently caress her breast. Suddenly, within an instant, our bodies intertwine in a love dance.

With her body sprawled across my desk, her legs spread open wide—I thrust myself into her. "Oh," she moans sexually, "Oh God." Her moaning becomes more intense by each stroke as she pulls me closer grinding her pelvis upon me—eyes rolling to the back of her head—fingernails clawing my back. "I'm coming, oh God," she says heavily breathing, "Oh, God." With moments to spare, I explode in her.

"Oh baby, that was wonderful," she says as she stares into my eyes. "We need to do this more often." Thinking to myself how great that would be as I remove myself from within her, "That would be great," I say nervously rushing to get my clothes intact, "but we can't keep meeting like this." Pausing to gather my thoughts before I slip up and say the wrong thing, I stutter, "I mean, just not at my place of employment."

She seductively rises up from the desk and adjusts my tie, "you haven't said anything before," she says, "what—you don't like the spontaneity anymore?"

"Yes I do, but we can't keep this up," I say while slowly backing off her, "somebody's liable to get hurt." She looks at me with this blank stare as if I've just broken her heart. And the truth of the matter is, I did.

"What do you mean, somebody's liable to get hurt?" she asks, "you know what we agreed on when we met, no strings attached. So if anybody's going to get hurt, it will be the person who gets all emotional and falls in love." Trying not to be so obvious, I conceal my laughter and reply, "I know what we agreed on, but it won't be me. If anybody's going to get hurt, it may be you."

She looks at me perturbed, "Me?! Get my emotions involved? Please, I'm not the one who wants a wife and family," she says.

"Well, we can't keep meeting under these conditions, this thing that we're doing, we can't keep this up." I say nervously while adjusting my tie. "And what is this thing that we can't keep up?" she asks with a look of uncertainty. Lost for words, I couldn't gather myself to tell her that I just couldn't continue meeting with her based on the merits of sex alone, and that I do want more from her than just sex. "What's wrong, Danny, are you developing feelings for me?" she asks with brisk sarcasm.

"No, I'm just saying," I reply. She turns and looks at me in a state of confusion, "Saying what, Mr. Armstrong?" Adjusting my slacks, I'm hesitant to respond, "I'm just saying if we keep this up, someone will develop feelings, so we may need to stop meeting like this before someone gets hurt."

She walks toward me and plants a kiss on my lips, "Like who?" Although she and I have an understanding of what we share, the new Danny Armstrong wanted more than just sex out of a relationship. I wanted a partner, someone I could grow old with and raise a family. But never did I think she would be the one to give me what I wanted.

#

It was January 19, 2003, Brianna Denise Armstrong was born weighing in at 8 lbs, 4 oz. and 42 inches, to the proud parents of Danny Armstrong and Sonya Good, of whom neither was ready for a baby, or at least I wasn't. The fact that I was now a proud father took some time to sink in. That's when reality hit me and my way of living life in the fast lane partying almost every weekend, dating multiple women, and living the single life was altered in just a matter of seconds. At the brink of my success as a rising young business mogul, I was now a father with bigger priorities and a series of issues to contend with Sonya. I come to discover that she had an alternative motive—to capture me in a lover's squall, I never intended on being in.

Caught in a love affair of mixed emotions, I'm trapped and held hostage to Sonya's manipulation—and Brianna is the star of her scheme.

The Plot Thickens

www.ingramcontent.com/pod-product-compliance
Lightning Source LLC
Chambersburg PA
CBHW060140130626
46556CB00006B/2426